CONSUMED BY TRUTHS

TRUTH OR LIES BOOK 6

ELLA MILES

PROLOGUE

KAI

I THOUGHT death was my greatest enemy.

I thought nothing could be worse.

I thought death was the ultimate end.

I couldn't be more wrong.

Death isn't the end.

It isn't the enemy.

At least, that's what I keep telling myself.

Death isn't what broke my heart—Enzo did.

He's broken my heart so many times before.

He's let me down.

Let me get hurt.

But those times were nothing compared to how I feel now—that pain was nothing.

Because when he broke my heart before, we weren't in love. We didn't have a child on the way. We weren't facing our greatest enemy.

I'm not mad. It's not Enzo's fault he couldn't stay away. It's not his fault he didn't know the risks. It's not his fault he didn't know why I hid away, pretending to be dead.

But of course, Enzo found me.

How could he not?

We've been drawn together from the start. Like two trains on a collision course. We've been going full speed toward each other, damn the consequences. Somehow, we've managed to avoid the derailment, the explosion, the end. But we can't avoid it anymore. We can't stop ourselves from colliding.

We've both tried applying the brakes. We've tried heading in different directions. But somehow, we always find our way back to the other.

And when we meet, it's not a gentle embrace; we mix together like fire and ice. And the quake we cause can be felt for miles around.

We aren't good for each other.

We aren't good for our baby.

We aren't good for the company.

We aren't good for the world.

But that doesn't stop us.

Nothing can. We can't stop ourselves.

Both of us have tried to stop loving the other. We've pretended to hate each other. We've tried living apart. But we can't. Our attraction to each other is too great.

But I thought this time, we'd remain apart. I thought the illusion of death would separate us. That's what's in wedding vows after all: '...til death do us part.'

Death is supposed to be the end.

It's supposed to part us.

But in this case, death didn't part us. It didn't end us. Our love is too great for death to get in the way.

Enzo found me.

He found me.

I was dead.

But it didn't stop him from searching. It didn't stop him

from feeling me everywhere. It didn't stop him from loving me.

The problem with love like ours is that it is all-consuming.

We can't think, breathe, or exist without the other.

We need our love to live.

So Enzo didn't have a choice but to find me. He couldn't live without me. And I was barely living without him.

He found me.

I should have been ecstatic. Jumping for joy. Floating on a cloud. Feeling all the cheesy metaphors.

My heart should have been whole. Instead, he broke it deeper.

The only thing keeping my heart beating was that I had finally found a way to protect all the people I loved. I was protecting my baby and protecting Enzo.

But then Enzo returned, crashing back into my life, and I knew we would never be the same.

Death isn't the end. Nothing can keep Enzo and me apart.

But the world is going to wish that death did. That we were truly over and gone. Because Enzo is about to set the globe on fire with our vengeance, and I'm going to turn anyone in our way into ice.

Because even though my heart is breaking, knowing I can't protect Enzo, it won't stop me from taking on the world to meld our hearts together. Mine is forever broken without Enzo. And I've realized the only way to heal is to put our broken pieces together.

The world may wish I had stayed dead. But the world should have known there is no killing a love like ours.

One of us must die, so the other can live.

The words of my father haunt me.

But I don't fear them anymore.

Because dying to protect the man I love is exactly how our story should end—not with a happily ever after. Such a thing doesn't exist in our world. Our love story ends with sacrifice, an epic end.

A finale only our love is worthy of.

1

ENZO

THE WORLD HAS GONE DARK.

Like the entire world decided to flick off their lightswitches all at the same time, and agreed to never turn them back on. All I've seen for weeks is darkness.

There is no electricity.

No light guiding my way.

Not even a sunrise to greet me in the morning.

The world is dark.

Or maybe the world hasn't literally turned the lights off. I'm sure the sun has risen. If not, we'd all be dead, but I haven't seen it. I have a filter over my eyes. A haze that prevents me from seeing the light.

My mother is gone.

My father is gone.

Pietro and Milo are gone.

Zeke is gone.

Liesel is gone.

Langston is gone.

I'm familiar with death. Used to losing those I love. That

list is short compared to the countless number of men and women who have died fighting to protect me.

I should be used to dealing with death.

But I don't think death is something that anyone really gets used to. Because each death of someone you love leaves a permanent mark on your soul. A black spot you can never remove. And from my short list of loved ones alone, my soul must be mostly black at this point.

None of those deaths cast my soul into permanent blackness, however. Because only one person matters. My heart beats for only one person, even though she's gone. My heart will never stop being hers.

Kai.

Kai is gone.

Our child—gone.

She's everything I've been fighting for. Everything I've done has been for her.

And now she's gone.

No, not gone. That word implies she will return. That she is simply off somewhere on vacation and will return one day.

Kai is dead.

Dead—I've never hated a word so much.

But I'm not going to war against the word. I'm going to war against the world.

Because the world let her die. The world didn't protect her. The world had the most beautiful, strong woman, and it let her die.

I slam my hand hard down into the wheel of the yacht I'm driving. I hear the bones crunch, the tendons snap, and blood explode beneath my skin. But I don't feel the pain.

I'm numb to pain. Because I'm not mad at the world, I'm mad at myself.

I failed Kai—again.

I've failed so many fucking times.

So many times.

But I won't again.

Because I can't fail her anymore.

She's dead.

There is nothing left to protect.

No one left to save.

If I thought killing myself would be enough to avenge her death, I would already be dead. But it's not enough. I may not have been able to protect her, not strong enough to save her. But then, saving others was never my strongest skill.

I learned a long time ago how to live in the shadows. Not just live, but thrive. Now that there is no more light in my world, I will flourish. I will slink through the darkness. I am a ghost. No one will see me coming. I will kill every person who let this happen.

Felix is at the top of my list, but he will be the last to die. He thinks he doesn't fear death. He doesn't—not now. Because he has nothing to lose. Nothing he loves left.

So I will wait. I'll be patient. I'll watch, stalk him like he stalked me. I will wait until he falls in love. And then I will take it from him. Only then will he fear death. Not his own, but of the person he loves.

Everyone else though—his team, my own crew that followed him instead of being loyal to me—they are all fair game. And I will enjoy the hunt.

The world will burn, that will be the only light I see in the weeks to come. The light of my fire will be all I leave behind.

I've been sailing this yacht for weeks. Chasing cowards as they run for the farthest, most distant places on Earth.

They can run. But I will find them. All of them. And they will pay for what they did. For their betrayal. For their disloyalty. They will all pay the ultimate price.

I grip the wheel tighter as the rain comes down in sheets. The waves rock high then low. And the wind does its best to flip my ship over—*not going to happen.*

I've had years of experience steering a boat. I've faced the worst storms imaginable. The weather won't stop me.

Most sailors would say you should never take to the ocean alone. You have no idea what dangers you will face. You have no idea how the tides will turn against you.

But after what happened, I prefer to be alone. I can't trust anyone, not anymore. Everyone I ever trusted is dead.

From now on, I do everything alone. I can't trust anyone else so I won't. I don't need anyone but me.

I can move much faster on my own. I can disappear into the shadows if I'm just one person. And I don't have to worry if the men and women who work for me are on my side or not.

I'm sure Archard survived. I'm sure he'll come at me with contracts and papers, trying to get me to complete the final task so I can earn the rightful title of Mr. Black, ruler of an empire of men, women, weapons, technology, ships.

I don't want any of it. I will never trust a person again. I will never trust my own team to be loyal to me. And I don't need any new weapons or technology to kill those who have betrayed me.

And I sure as hell don't need the money.

If Archard comes anywhere near me with contracts and rules about taking over as Black, I'll kill him.

I'm already Black—Enzo Black. I was born Enzo Black, and I'll die Enzo Black. I don't need to win a fucking competition and jump through hoops like a circus animal in order to lay claim to my own last name.

Felix wants the empire. He wants to rule the men. He craves the power. But I'm going to destroy everything, so there will be nothing left for him to rule.

I spot a ship in the distance. The sky is dark, and so is the ocean. The rain still falls hard, which should make it impossible to see, but I know it's one of my yachts.

The yacht is dark, with no lights on, but I can see the outline of it through the dark. I can see the Black name etched on the side. But more than what I can see, I have a gut feeling deep inside that this is one of my yachts. And that is what guides me.

I shut off my own engine—a risky move considering I won't be able to steer without the engines running. I'll be at the mercy of the waves as I drift closer to the other boat. But somehow I think the ocean is on my side tonight.

The ocean and I have always gotten along—partly because I respected it and never tried to conquer it like most men do. But tonight I'm going to test that relationship more than I ever have.

The storm coming down all around me could mean my end. But I don't fear death. I welcome it.

I descend flights of stairs to the room that should be my bedroom, although I can't recall the last time I've slept. Instead, I pass out wherever I sit with a bottle of whiskey in my hand.

But tonight, I might sleep well for the first time in weeks. Because tonight, I get my first taste of revenge.

My bed is covered in weapons—guns, knives, bullets. I load up my favorite guns and ensure the knives have been sharpened.

Each time I grab for a weapon, I see the scrunchie

around my wrist. The only thing left of Kai is a scrunchie she wore to remember a different man. A wooden heart I carved for her hangs from it.

The scrunchie represents so much more than my loss of Kai or Zeke. It represents everything taken from me. This scrunchie was never meant to be more than a nice gesture that Zeke gave to Kai. Something to keep her hair back while she fought. It wasn't meant to be carried around everywhere like a memorial.

But somehow everything we have ever given each other becomes a memorial to the dead. Everyone in my life dies; that's the one thing I know for sure. It's why I know my enemies will die.

I feel the fabric of the scrunchie between my thumb and finger.

"I will not fail you," I say. *I won't fail any of them.*

I run up the stairs, armed with weapons and a broken heart beating for revenge.

The yacht rocks, the kind of rocking that should knock me on my ass, but my feet are too steady to let something that simple derail me.

My boots hit the open top deck, drenched in rain, the wind trying to push me back down. But I don't move.

Do your best rain. Nothing can fucking stop me.

I peer through the rain to the other yacht. The engines are still running, but whoever is steering it has little or no experience steering a boat through weather like this.

I grin.

I have the advantage.

I walk to the edge of my yacht. I consider jumping in and swimming to the other yacht. I'm a good enough swimmer, and I feel like, for the first time ever, the world is on my side. The weather may be trying to fight against me, but it's actually helping me. Because I can handle the weather—they can't.

I have a different idea in mind. One that won't involve me drinking a crap ton of saltwater.

I head back to the helm. I fire up the engines and start driving toward the doomed ship.

I never thought I would ram one of my own ships, but that seems to be the direction I'm headed in.

At least I'll make them think I'm willing to ram my own ship.

I turn my lights on full force, ensuring they see the devil heading straight toward them. They will know I'm coming, and there is nothing they can do about it.

Faster my yacht drives toward theirs. Closer, closer. I see men huddled together on the bridge. All bickering and grabbing the helm randomly trying to fight the waves to get out of my way. But there is nothing they can do to stop me from coming for them. For every single one of them.

When I'm close enough that the collision is inevitable, I let go of the wheel and march out into the rain. So they can see clearly who their attacker is.

The impact hits.

Our yachts slam into each other with a loud screech—the sound of scraping metal rings in the air.

The sound soothes my broken soul. I don't even care about my precious yachts anymore. They all deserve to be cast down to the depths of the ocean. I even blame my ships for Kai's death. They didn't save her either.

I watch as men fall overboard into the choppy water, most likely to their deaths.

Men I would have jumped into the water to save before. They were my crew. I would have risked my life for them; I would have died for them.

But now, I wouldn't risk my pinky finger to save them.

I walk forward to where our ships are locked together. I step across the gap and onto their ship. The sky still rains down on me; the wind whips through me. I should be freezing from chilled water; instead, I burn of fire.

I walk straight to the bridge, calmly withdraw my favorite gun, and fire.

The rain makes it easier for me to kill them. I shoot them dead before they can even lift their weapons in my direction. But it makes each kill less personal, and this is as personal as it gets.

I should torture each and every one of them before I kill them. But I don't have the energy. And I have far too many men to kill to waste time with torture.

I fire over and over—through the rain.

The only indications I've hit my targets are when each man falls to the ground in a heap.

Not one man has fired back at me.

Not one man has fought back.

I feel invincible in this moment. Maybe I'm really not capable of dying. Which would be a shame since I feel like dying. I need the end to come. I need to return to the ground, or maybe the sea—become worm or fish food.

I march into the boat's decks, taking out man after man. The rain no longer provides me cover in the depths of the ship, so a few men get shots off before they succumb. But they all die.

I step over a body as I walk to the back of the ship, where I find no more traitors. Everyone is dead.

I walk through the entire ship twice, ensuring I didn't miss a single person.

Finally, I'm satisfied no one escaped my wrath. But I don't feel any weight lifting. I thought that killing those who betrayed us would make me feel better, even a minuscule amount better. But it didn't.

There is no recovering from this kind of heartbreak. Nothing will make me feel better. I'm not doing this to heal. I'm doing this for Kai. For my baby.

I crack my neck back and forth, trying to release the tension I feel as I put my gun back into my pants. I didn't even have to draw a second gun. Or pull out a knife.

It was too easy.

How disappointing.

I want a fight—a battle. I want to feel something—even if it's rage.

I walk back up onto the top deck, the rain has started to lighten, as if it knows it is no longer necessary to pour down because everyone is dead.

I stare at the two yachts both damaged from the impact. It's going to be hard to steer either one out of this storm.

I sigh.

Might as well get to work trying to separate them and see which one has less damage.

But then I see something.

A flicker of a shadow through the rain.

Felix—my gut says.

I had planned on waiting to kill him. Take my time; only kill him when I would do the most damage to him possible. But he's here, right in front of me.

I won't be waiting. The rage beats through my body.

This ends. Now.

Lighting strikes the ship, setting the rear on fire.

I grin.

The weather is again on my side.

The rain drums down harder again, but it makes no

impact on the fire. The fire will burn until there is nothing left for either of us to stand on, but I don't care.

I might be dead, but so will Felix.

This will end.

I think the shadow is going to disappear into the ship—Felix is a slimy coward after all.

But he doesn't.

Instead, he stands taller. His eyes are squinting in my direction. And then a cold smile curls up. He wants this to be over too.

He's going to fight me.

I lift my gun.

He does too.

The crack of us both firing our guns sounds like lightning booming through the sky. Maybe it is actually lightning and thunder. It makes no difference.

Bullets travel, but neither of us hit the other.

I fire again and again. My aim perfect, but the rain and wind get in my way. The bullets no longer travel straight into the heart of my targets.

Which somehow makes me happy. I don't want Felix to end with a single bullet—that would be too easy.

But it still fuels my rage to shoot bullet after bullet in his direction. And it seems it does the same to him, because he continues to fire back.

Until a crack of thunder changes both of our minds at the same time.

This is too personal to be fought with guns.

We run—head first into each other.

The collision seems to spark another crack of lightning as if the storm is reacting to our fight. Like there is something bigger happening than just the fight between the two of us.

Our fists hit—jaws, stomachs, eyes.

Both of us try to do as much damage as possible. Each time my fist connects with him—I feel more alive. This is the reason I survived when Kai didn't. To get revenge. To kill this monster. And each punch of his fist connecting with my flesh ignites more testosterone flowing through my body.

Felix will not win.

We both flip over each other, driving each other's bodies into various objects on the ship. Everything is a weapon. And both of us are willing to fight dirty.

I have Felix in a chokehold. He can't go anywhere. I'll suffocate him before I let him go. I win.

But then he kicks his legs up, throwing his body back on mine, we crash to the floor, and I have no option but to let go.

It's a move I know well. I invented it for just this kind of situation. But it's not a move my father taught me. It's not one Felix would have learned from our father.

I created the move.

It's counter-intuitive to what you want to do when you are trapped and fighting for a breath. You sacrifice your body, surprising your opponent, and in turn, it allows you to again have the upper hand.

I've only taught the move to two men. Two men who I thought were dead—Langston and Zeke.

But one of them is alive.

I thought I was fighting Felix—my enemy.

I was wrong. I'm fighting my only friend still alive in the world. I thought everyone I loved was dead. I had given up hope. But sometimes people return from the dead.

2

KAI

Days.

Weeks.

Years.

I can't tell the difference anymore. All I know is time is passing too slowly and too quickly. I'm never going to survive if the days continue on like this.

The only way I know time is passing at all is my growing bump. It seems every time I look down at it, it has doubled in size. I feel huge, like I have a giant bowling ball in my belly. I know it isn't that big yet, but tell that to my back, which aches and agonizes. All I ever do is move between the bed, couch, and rocking chair on the back deck.

Right now, I'm in the rocking chair.

Gliding it back and forth as I stare out at the Alaskan wilderness. It's the middle of summer here, which means the air is a warm seventy-five degrees. I can't imagine what winters are going to be like here. I plan on surviving by burying myself under a pile of blankets and never leaving the house until summer returns.

Or I could leave? Find somewhere else to live?

Not going to happen. This is the best hiding place, because no one would ever expect me to have sought out my dad.

No, I'll stay.

My father—scratch that—my uncle, walks out onto the back porch carrying a tray of orange juice, bacon, eggs, and toast. He never once made me breakfast while I was growing up. But now he won't let me skip a meal. I blame him for my belly doubling in size in the few weeks I've been here.

He sets the tray down on the table between the two rocking chairs.

"Any news about Enzo?" I ask.

My uncle freezes for only a moment, and then he hands me a glass of orange juice.

I take it, but I'm not letting him off the hook. If I'm going to survive a life without Enzo, then I need as many updates as I can get about him.

"No."

I growl. "What use are you if you aren't going to do the one thing I need? I need updates on Enzo."

"No, you don't."

I glare at my uncle. "Yes, I do! You have no idea how hard this is on me."

My uncle gets right in my face, scolding me like I'm a child. Maybe I am. Maybe I shouldn't be acting out. But I can't help it. I need Enzo. I need to know he's alive. I need to know what he's doing. What he's thinking. Does he know I'm alive? Is his heart broken? What's happening?

"Listen to me, Katherine," my uncle says.

"Kai," I hiss. "My name is Kai."

"Kai, listen to me." He grabs my shoulders and softens his voice. "I'm sorry. I know how hard it is not to have answers. I've been living here for months without knowing if you were alive or not. If you had won the game or not. When someone you love is out there, and you don't get to know anything about them, it's like you are slowly suffocating from the inside out. You can't eat, breathe, or think without knowing if that person is alive. I understand."

I shake my head as a tear drips. "You don't love me, uncle. You made me live like we had no money. You sold me like cattle, instead of telling me the truth and preparing me for a battle I wasn't ready to face. You don't love me, uncle."

He winces every time I say the word, *uncle.*

"You can love someone and still fuck up. I thought you of all people would know that."

I narrow my eyes as the anger penetrates again. "What do you mean, I of all people should know that?"

He sighs as if he realized he fucked up again. "I just meant the man you love, and are desperate to find out even the smallest piece of information about, has also sold you, has he not?"

I'm going to kill my uncle. I'm going to kill him.

And I let him know that with my gaze, my flared nostrils, my clenched jaw, and my tight fists.

"Enzo loves me. This isn't about Enzo. This is about you loving me. This is about your screw-ups."

My uncle nods. "You're right. I'm not trying to say I didn't fuck up. I did—in the worst possible way. I was a mess after your father died. I thought I could have saved him. I thought it should have been me that died. And then your mother died. And I was left with you—the only piece left of either one of them. And I did everything I could think of to protect you. I made you as strong as possible. The men that kidnapped you, initially they were supposed to just take you to some far off island to live comfortably where you would be safe. But then Enzo's father found out. And so I turned it into an opportunity to make you stronger, strong enough to survive."

"Well, great fucking job," I say sarcastically. "I'm strong and broken and completely fucked up. And in the end, I'm still hiding away from reality."

I look away; I can't look at my uncle any longer. I can't keep doing this for days, weeks, years. I need another solution.

My uncle stands up, clear that this conversation is over. Ending like every other conversation we've had—in a fight.

"I can't ask my contacts about Enzo on a regular basis. They would get suspicious. They will investigate me. They will find you here. And then your sacrifice will be for nothing."

Tears fall hard now—*damn pregnancy hormones*. I cry at the smallest of things now. Although, I'm not sure I can blame this one on pregnancy hormones.

My uncle leaves without another word. He doesn't try to comfort me, not that I would let him.

I stare at the tray of food next to me. I've lost my appetite. I haven't heard any news about Enzo in weeks. And I won't be getting any updates. This is my life now.

I'm dead.

I feel dead.

Even though I'm staring out at an extraordinary view of the wilderness, I see nothing but dark shadows. Everything is in shades of gray. I don't see color anymore.

I know birds are singing happily in a nearby tree, but the sound isn't pleasant. It sounds like nails on a chalkboard to my ears.

There is a delicious plate of food next to me. I should crave it. I should want to eat every bite, if for no other reason than to provide nourishment for my baby. Instead, it smells as good to eat as sewage.

I want to sleep.

So that's what I do.

I head inside and find my bedroom. The only bedroom in this house. My uncle has been sleeping on the couch since I got here. And when the baby comes...I have no idea. But my brain can't focus on planning. My heart doesn't dance at the upcoming arrival of my baby.

I'm numb.

I'm broken.

I'm dead.

I close my eyes. Letting sleep take over.

———

I SEE HIM—ENZO *Black.*

He's standing at the foot of my bed.

I pinch myself. I'm not dreaming. This is real. He's here!

"Enzo!" I yell, sitting up in the bed.

He grins but shushes me.

"Sorry," I half-whisper, half-yell. I can't help myself. He's here.

He's here, but he hasn't hugged me yet. Or kissed me. Or touched me. And I can't wait for him to move the few feet toward me.

I jump out of bed, trying not to trip over my own feet as I run into his arms. But of course, he catches me, so there is no reason to worry about falling.

His arms are stronger and rougher than I remember, but it's just because I haven't felt his arms around me in so long. I hold him tighter, fighting back tears.

"You came," I say.

"Of course I came, stingray."

I step back. "You shouldn't have come. It's not safe. If Felix or the crew find out we are both alive, they will kill one of us..."

"I know."

My eyes widen.

"Then why are you here?"

"I couldn't stay away. I love you. Our love will triumph over anything."

I nod. He's right. Of course, he's right. Why did I worry?

I wrap my arms tighter around him. I'm safe. Our baby is safe. Enzo is safe. We are all safe.

But I know better than to think we are safe when we aren't.

My uncle enters.

"You shouldn't be here," my uncle yells to Enzo.

"Enzo is exactly where he should be," I yell back.

My uncle grabs Enzo's arm, pulling him from me.

"No! Don't take him! I love him!" I yell.

But it doesn't stop my uncle. He rips Enzo from my arms.

"No!" my fists start flying, slamming into my uncle over and over. "Let him go!"

But my uncle already has Enzo. And then he raises a gun and pulls the trigger.

———

I WAKE up on the floor covered in sweat, panting heavily, with my arms wrapped around the dresser as it starts to tumble on top of me. My uncle is standing over me, holding the dresser back.

"It was just a nightmare," my uncle says, pushing the dresser back against the wall.

My uncle kneels down in front of me. "It was just a nightmare," he repeats, knowing I need to hear it.

I nod. "A nightmare."

I close my eyes as I tremble. *It was just a nightmare. Enzo is safe. He's just not here.*

My uncle touches my hand gently.

I open my eyes.

"Do you think you can get back into bed and try to sleep?" he asks.

I shake my head. I know I won't be getting any sleep for a while.

He nods and then holds out his hand.

I stare at it like it's a snake that will probably bite me. But I take his hand, as I could use the help getting up off the floor. He pulls me up.

"I'll make you some tea," he says before leaving.

I stare around the room. *How long have I been asleep?* It's light outside. I don't remember falling asleep. I don't remember waking up. I don't remember anything but that dream.

I grab my robe and tie it around my waist before I head out to drink some tea and try to calm my nerves.

I step into the kitchen and then freeze.

My uncle isn't alone. He invited someone else into the house.

Not just someone else—a man. A handsome man, maybe late twenties, with a scruffy beard, dreamy eyes, and a white pearly smile. He's wearing jeans and a buttoned-down shirt with the sleeves rolled up. He kind of looks like a sexy lumberjack.

"Who are you?" I ask, as I take a seat at the bar next to the man, doing my best to give him an unfriendly glare that tells him to get the fuck out of my house as soon as possible.

The man grins at me, clearly not reading too much into my angry scowl.

"I'm Beckett," he holds out his hand, expecting me to shake it.

I raise an eyebrow and glance from him to my uncle. "I need more than a name. Like what the hell you are doing in my house?"

My uncle gives me a scowl before putting my cup of tea in front of me.

The man chuckles, like he finds me hilarious instead of mean and angry. Not the reaction I was hoping for. I want him to run as far and fast as he can away from me.

"I work with your father."

I look to my 'father' as I have no idea what his job is or that he works. "And what exactly do you do for work?"

"We are fisherman," Beckett answers. "There aren't many other jobs you can do around here."

"Of course, you're fishermen." I study Beckett and then my father. "So fisherman Beckett, you still haven't told me what you are doing in my house so early in the morning?"

He cocks his head, flashing his perfect dimple and straight teeth that I'm sure most woman fall for. But I'm not most women. I'm not falling for it. If this man is friends with my uncle, then he's dangerous.

"First, it's the middle of the afternoon," Beckett says, eyeing my robe like I'm the crazy one.

"Oh. Well, I sleep crazy hours now that I'm pregnant."

If that doesn't scare the man off, nothing will.

It doesn't scare him off.

"I completely understand. I'm just here to watch the game with your father."

"Game? My father doesn't watch games."

Beckett shrugs. "I'm originally from St. Louis; I'm a huge Cardinals fan."

"Still doesn't explain what you are doing here? Don't you have your own television to watch the game on?"

"No, actually," Beckett grins.

My father shrugs and walks over to the living room; he hands Beckett a beer.

"You should eat, Katherine. I've made all your favorites and put them in the fridge," my uncle says before him and Beckett become engrossed in the game.

I walk over to the fridge because my stomach growls. My uncle doesn't know any of my favorite foods. But when I open the fridge and peer inside, I see all of my favorites—tacos, lasagna, macaroni and cheese, enchiladas.

I stare at my uncle sitting on the couch with Beckett. I really don't understand him. *Could he have really had a change of heart?*

I warm up the lasagna and decide to watch the game with them. It will distract me from my nightmare.

The game is boring.

Beckett tries to make jokes. I think he's flirting, but I can't be sure as I haven't had another man flirt with me in a long time. But the more he flirts, the angrier I get.

My uncle keeps smiling smugly between the two of us every time Beckett says something funny or gets me to crack the tiniest of smiles. I will admit, Beckett is funny. And I get a warm feeling when I'm around him. But he's nothing compared to Enzo.

The game finally ends.

"Well, that was boring. Thanks for coming over to watch the game, Beckett. Don't bother coming over to watch the game again. We won't be watching any more Cardinals games," I say, trying to be as mean and snarky as possible.

Of course, it just makes mister smiley grin. "I had a good time too, Kai."

He called me, Kai, not Katherine, even though my uncle called me Katherine the entire time we were watching the game. My suspicions are growing about this guy.

"Goodbye, Beckett," I say.

"Goodbye, Kai."

Beckett leaves. I walk to the door and look into the peep-hole to make sure he leaves.

And then I turn my anger on my uncle.

"What the hell was that?" I yell.

My uncle narrows his eyes. "You are going to have to be more specific with what you are angry with me about. Since you are angry with me about everything lately."

"Beckett. Why did you invite him over?"

"Because you had been asleep for three days, and he's my friend, and I knew he wanted to watch the game, so I invited him over. It's my house, and I wasn't sure if you were going to leave your bedroom or not."

I glare. "Why did you invite him over? Does her work for the Black organization?"

"What? Of course not."

I cross my arms. "Then why did you invite him over? Was that a setup? A date?"

My uncle doesn't answer, which means I'm right.

I throw my head back and my arms ups. "I give up. I shouldn't have come back here. I should have gone some-where by myself. You are unbelievable. Trying to set me up while I'm pregnant with another man's baby."

I start storming off to my bedroom, intent on packing. But my uncle steps in the way.

"What are you doing? Get out of my way," I huff.

He shakes his head. "You deserve a life, Kai. A life where you get to be happy. I didn't set you up on that date because I thought Beckett was the right man for you or that you are anywhere near ready to move on. I'm just trying to show you there is a life outside these walls. That even though you are running, and can never be with the man you want, you can be with a man again. You can find a man who will make you happy, a man who can make you laugh, a man you call fall in love with."

"I can't fall in love. Not when I'm in love with Enzo. My heart belongs to him. I don't want it back."

My uncle stiffens. "Maybe—maybe you can only form a friendship. Maybe it will be love but not as intense as what you have with Enzo. But you need to move on. You need to be happy. You need to start planning for the future."

"I can't," I sob.

My uncle wraps me in his arms, pulling me to him. I'm too tired to protest or stop him. And I need the hug.

"You can. You are the strongest person I know. And maybe that's my fault, but I think you would have turned out this way despite my stupid intervention. You have to live. You have to fight. You have to find something worth living for. Otherwise, you will die in this house. I can't bring you out of the fog, my daughter; you have to do that on your own."

Daughter.

More tears.

My uncle loves me. And he still sees me as his daughter. No matter how badly he messed up before.

"Are you going to live or die? Because I can't stand by and watch my daughter dissolve into nothing. I know Enzo is the love of your life. You deserve a lifetime of happiness with him. But you made your decision. You chose to save all three of you: Enzo, the baby, and yourself. You made the strong choice, but you have to keep making the strong choice every single day.

"Your love story is epic and unstoppable. Nothing will diminish your love for Enzo. But you have to find a way to live with the hurt. Find someone else you can love, even if that love isn't as strong."

I nod into my father's chest—*father*. He may have fucked up a lot, but as he holds me, I know he loves me. I know he still sees himself as my father. I don't forgive him for everything he's done. But I do trust him now.

And then I feel it.

The fluttering in my stomach. Like tiny little butterflies.

I pull back and grip my stomach.

"Kai, what's wrong?"

The fluttering gets harder, more like light thumps.

I grin as I bite my bottom lip. Then I grab my father's hand and place it over my stomach.

And then our tears are falling hard. Beautiful, crocodile tears that run down our cheeks and over our large grins.

"The baby is kicking," I say, with a light laugh.

"It's incredible," my father says.

I nod and close my eyes as I hold my father's hand over my stomach, and the fluttering continues. My father saved the baby. And my baby reminded me I do have something to live for—or rather, someone.

Until this moment, the baby didn't feel real. And I had my doubts about it being Enzo's. But now, I know as the warmth spreads all over my body from the inside out. The same warm feeling I get when Enzo touches me. This baby is his. The warmth is his. And I don't need to replace the love I feel for Enzo with something new. I just need to open my heart, widen my love to include our baby as well. And right now, I've never felt a greater love than that of the baby I created with the love of my life.

3

ENZO

"LANGSTON?" I ask.

The man on top of me freezes as I say his name.

My heart pounds. I've imagined so many fucking times a person I love coming back to life. That I got it wrong. That they weren't dead, just gone—hiding, waiting until the threat was gone to reappear. I've dreamed of this moment so many times. But every time I did, I would wake up. And I would realize the dream wasn't real.

This feels real.

I feel the rain dripping down on top of us. The wind knocking through our bodies. His weight on top of me.

But that doesn't mean anything. All of my dreams before were vivid. All of them I thought were real.

This is just a dream, I tell myself. *Don't get your hopes up.* The devastation that will come when you wake up will be all too much.

The man doesn't answer.

Maybe I was wrong? Maybe I'm imagining things because I hoped so much for any person I cared about to come back? I'm putting other people's faces on my enemies.

No.

I know in my heart the man on top of me is Langston.

I just don't know yet if this is a dream or reality.

"Langston," I say more affirmatively.

I loosen my grip on his neck, trying to show I don't want to hurt him.

The man on top of me shows me no such mercy. He jabs his elbow hard into my stomach and then slices a knife across my neck before I can react.

The cut isn't deep, just enough to spill blood. But it still hurts like a motherfucker.

Langston turns, looking me in the eyes.

I grin. *He's here. He's alive.* And I know from the intensity of the cut that this is real. This isn't a dream.

"Langston," I breathe, as tears stream. I never thought I'd see him again. And the emotions I feel overwhelm me. "You're alive."

"And you aren't real," Langston says.

He begins to jab the knife into my neck again, but this time I block him, even through my tears.

"Langston, it's me, Enzo."

He shakes his head. "Enzo is dead."

I kick Langston off of me, and hold my hands out cautiously, like I'm trying to approach a lion about to attack me. Langston still grips the knife in his hand. I don't doubt he has a gun he will pull on me soon.

I don't want to shoot or stab him. I just need to knock him out of whatever nightmare he is going through.

I look him over for the first time as the rain softens around us. He's wearing jeans heavily stained black and red. His black shirt has more holes in it than not. He hasn't shaved in weeks. His hair is ragged and growing around his ears. But none of that is what worries me—it's the look in his eyes.

Langston has given up. He thinks everyone he loves is dead—I know the feeling. He looks like complete devastation and death. There is no light behind his eyes. No reason to live. Not even for revenge. He's just going through the motions. He's not really here.

He's with Liesel, and Kai, and Zeke. His heart is gone. He thinks I'm a figment of his imagination. His dreams playing tricks on him again—I can't really be here.

"This isn't a dream, Langston. This is real," I shout over the howling wind and rain never ceasing. The ship continues to burn around us, and soon will fall to the depths of the ocean.

"Liar. You're dead," Langston says, his voice relaxed and monotone.

I hold my hands up. "Would your enemies hold their hands up like this?"

"You aren't my enemy. You're my nightmare," Langston says.

"Ask me. Ask me something only I would know. Something that would make you feel this is real and not a dream," I say.

He considers for a moment. "In high school, you said Jessica Willis kissed you, not the other way around. Was it true?"

"No, I kissed her. I knew you liked her, and I betrayed you. I'm sorry."

Langston shakes his head.

I slowly put my hands down, hoping this is over. "You believe I'm real?"

He laughs. "No, the real Enzo would never admit to betraying me like that."

Fuck.

I see him reach for his gun at the same time I reach for my knife. I throw my knife before Langston has a chance to fire. The knife sticks into Langston's thigh.

He stares down at the wound, finally feeling more pain than a dream produces.

"This is real," I say, walking toward him.

He grabs the knife, pulls it out, and stares at the blood. "Real." Slowly, his eyes meet mine.

And then we embrace in a desperate hug.

"You're alive," Langston sobs into my shoulder.

"You're alive," I repeat, not believing my own words.

"How? You were dead," Langston says.

"I want to ask you the same question. Numerous people reported you dead. I saw the evidence. The security footage, there was no way you could have survived," I say.

He nods. "I shouldn't have."

"How did you?"

He shrugs. "Luck, determination. I'm not sure. I remember crawling away from the explosion. I ended up on the beach. And when I went back, everyone was gone or dead."

Langston's alive. *Could others be alive?*

Thump.

Thump.

Thump.

My heart speeds up at that, though. *Could Liesel be alive? Could Kai? The baby?*

"No," Langston says sternly.

"What?" I didn't ask him a question, so I don't know what he's answering.

"No, they aren't alive. Don't go there. Don't torture yourself."

"But—"

"No, I saw Liesel die. I saw Kai die. The baby—they are all gone. Don't torture yourself thinking they could be alive. They aren't."

He saw them die. They are really dead.

I step away, needing a moment.

"Don't do this to yourself. You seem in a healthier place than I am, don't let this change anything," Langston says.

"I'm in the healthier place? Really?"

But when I turn and look at Langston again, I know it's the truth. At least I've taken a shower and changed my clothes. I've eaten the occasional meal. I have a reason for existing—revenge.

Langston doesn't even seem to care about revenge. I don't think he's changed his clothes from that night. He's lost weight, so I doubt he's eaten more than the bare necessity to survive. His eyes are bloodshot, and his skin pale. Without intervention, I don't know how much longer he would survive.

But I see in him what only a person that has experienced a great love would see. Langston is heartbroken. Not because he thought he lost me or Kai even. But because he lost Liesel. He lost the love of his life, but unlike me, he never told her he loved her. He didn't kiss her lips. He didn't sink into her depths. He loved without ever saying it out loud, and now, it's too late.

I can't imagine the pain I would feel right now if I hadn't told Kai I loved her. If I hadn't gotten the limited time we had together.

It still should have been me instead. I should have been the one to die. But I know when she died, Kai knew what love felt like, and that was the greatest gift I could give her.

Langston is heartbroken in a way you can never heal

from. Never come to terms with. All the therapy in the world won't fix him. He will never recover from this. He may be alive, but my friend is gone. What is left is a shell of the man he once was.

"Join me," I hold my hand out to him.

He stares at it and then takes my hand, gripping it tightly. "Absolutely. We going to kill Felix for this?"

I nod. "Something like that."

———

"You good?" I ask Langston.

He nods. He hasn't spoken much in the three days we've been reunited. He's mostly in his own head. I basically had to shovel food into his mouth and throw him into a shower to get him fed and clean.

He's broken.

I'm broken.

And that makes us the most dangerous men alive. Because both of us will do whatever it takes to kill Felix. To kill everyone involved in Kai and Liesel's deaths.

"Do you understand the plan?" I ask.

He nods.

We stare at Milo and Felix's mansion in Italy. I used to think of it as only Milo's, but I realize now Felix was playing me the whole time pretending to be any other employee at Milo's organization, when in reality he had the same level of power as Milo.

"Good. They burned our club down. They burned our house down. Let's burn theirs," I say.

Langston's body tightens, but he doesn't react to my words.

I'm sure Felix isn't here. There aren't enough men

patrolling trying to protect him. I don't care that Felix isn't here. I want him to suffer. I want him to watch his home go up in flames like I had to. And I want to torture one of his men into giving me information about where Felix is.

Even though Felix doesn't have a lot of his men here, we are greatly outnumbered.

There are two of us.

Probably more than a dozen of them.

It's not my style to arm explosives and blow up my enemy without giving them a chance to hit me back. But after what Felix did, I'm more than happy to repay him the favor. He isn't the only one in this family who knows how to use explosives. And unlike him, I don't need the fanciest equipment or other people to do my dirty work.

I glance at Langston one last time. There was a time I would trust him with my life.

Do I trust him now? Is he stable enough to handle this?

Yes.

He may be heartbroken, but we've fought so many battles side by side I know what he's capable of. I know he fights almost automatically. He won't let his feelings cloud his judgment. He won't let his pain affect anything.

I have no doubts.

I give Langston the signal to brace himself, and then I press the button that will spark the explosion.

Nothing happens.

I press it again.

Nothing.

I look at Langston whose eyes have clouded over. He isn't here.

Fuck.

He was supposed to hook up the last explosives. He failed. He's not ready for this.

We should retreat.

But it's too late.

We've been spotted.

It's fight or die. And I'm not letting Langston die—not again. Even if he'd rather die to deal with his pain.

"Cover me," I say, hoping he can kill people from the bunker and not risk his own life, because if he hesitates for a second, he could die. And I won't survive watching him die.

I jump out of the bunker we are hiding in and start firing my weapon. I run away from Langston, trying to draw the enemy away from him.

It works.

Felix's men start chasing me.

I grin.

I'd rather take them down one by one than watch them die in an explosion anyway. But still, I want the house crumbling. I want the house burning. I want nothing left for Felix to return to.

One.

Two.

Three.

Three shots, three men down.

Four.

Five.

Six.

Three more down.

Seven.

Eight.

Nine.

All dead.

I counted twelve. Two are still chasing me, which means...

I turn back and see a man sneaking up on Langston from behind.

No!

I fire at the last two chasing me, confident that I got them and not giving them a second chance as I charge toward Langston. I yell for him to look behind him. To catch sight of what is happening, but it's all moving too fast.

I hear the shot.

I see Langston being hit.

And it's like watching him die all over again.

He should have stayed dead; I will never survive this pain.

4

KAI

"AND HOW DOES that make you feel?" my therapist asks.

My father suggested I see a therapist. Not to heal my relationship with him. I don't think our relationship is ever going to be fully salvageable, but because he thinks it will help me heal, move on. Deal with my new life.

I think my father is crazy. And if my therapist asks me one more time how I feel I'm going to kill him.

Maybe I should have gone to a female therapist? Maybe a woman would understand my situation better? But somehow I don't think so. I don't think a therapist has gone to enough years of training to understand the situation I've been through.

"Katherine, how does it make you feel?" Evan asks again.

Ugh, and don't get me started on him calling me Katherine. It was my father's idea. I know he's right. Kai is dead. I need to accept it. I need to go by an alias in case anyone comes looking for me. But I've always hated the name Katherine. Maybe I should choose another name, a name I actually like.

I stare across at my therapist, who now has a raised eyebrow as he waits for me to answer his question.

What was his question again?

Oh, right. It was how does losing the love of my life make me feel?

"Devastated," I say. *What else does he want me to say?* It feels like my heart was ripped from my chest. Like my soul was crushed. My will to live taken. My very existence squashed. But I choose only one word; I'm too exhausted to say more.

This is my second appointment for the day, having already been to the OBGYN, who basically yelled at me for not eating enough and set up an ultrasound for next week to check on the health of the baby. So now I'm eating, I'm taking my vitamins, I'm going to therapy to deal with my pain. I'm doing everything I can for this baby.

I just hope it's enough.

Evan frowns—clearly I said the wrong thing.

"I think we need to backtrack. You've lost a lot of people in your life. You've been betrayed by people you thought you loved. You've been hurt countless times. I think your pain is more than just about losing the man you loved. And I think letting go of that pain is going to be the hardest for you. You need to start smaller. Forgive someone of something smaller, let go of some smaller pain. Can you do that?"

Can I let go of something smaller? Let go of some other pain I'm dealing with?

Maybe.

But I'm more confident in front of my therapist. "Yes."

He smiles gently. Then reaches over to his side table and grabs a piece of paper with hearts all over it and a pen. He hands them both to me.

I raise an eyebrow at the heart stationary.

He grins and shrugs. "The hearts make the paper more special."

I nod.

"Write down something painful. Someone painful. Make it small. At least, smaller than letting go of the man you love. Write a goodbye. And let that pain go. Not to forget, but just so you can move on."

I nod.

I don't think I can. I don't think I can let any of the pain I'm feeling go, but I'll try.

The baby kicks again, and I wince.

At first, the kicks felt wonderful. Like tiny little butterflies, but each day the baby learns how to kick harder. The doctor said they shouldn't be painful yet, but I disagree. They are very painful.

Evan stares at me. "You okay?"

"Yes, just the baby is kicking."

"You are very brave, Katherine. And strong. You can do this, for your baby."

"Thank you."

I stand and walk out, armed with my paper and pen.

My father told me to text him, and he'd pick me up when I was done with my appointments, but I decide to take my therapist's advice. I walk down to the bridge overlooking a small creek.

This seems like the best place to let go of some pain.

But where to start?

My parents.

Zeke.

Langston.

Liesel.

Enzo.

None of them seem right to let go of. He said let go of the pain, not them.

I can do this.

I don't want to talk about my parent's deaths. I feel like I've already come to term with Zeke's death.

Langston.

My father gave me an update on this last week, but I wish he hadn't. Because he confirmed Langston and Liesel died that night. Enzo survived and has disappeared. But Langston and Liesel died.

Because of me—they are dead.

I couldn't save them.

I can save Enzo.

Langston—I have to let go of the pain I feel at his loss.

I write his name down at the top of the stationary with the hearts. And the rest just floods out of me...

———

"You don't have to hold my hair back every time I puke," I say.

He grins. "Yes, I do."

"No, you really don't. I'm disgusting and gross."

"Yes, you are."

I moan and then puke some more. "You are supposed to make me feel better, not agree with me." My head hangs over the toilet as Langston sits behind me, holding my hair back and rubbing my back.

He laughs. "Just a minute ago you were telling me I shouldn't even be here, but now you are telling me how to do my job."

"Yes," I say with a grin.

"Fine, you are beautiful, not disgusting. Is that better?"

"No," I smile.

"How about I tell you the truth?"

I roll my eyes. "Fine."

"The truth is I'm jealous."

"Jealous? Of my puke-fest?"

"Yes, despite what you think, you have a future. No matter what happens to you and Enzo, you have a part of that love you two have to take with you forever. You have a piece of him no one can take away. And yes, the result right now is puking over the toilet, with a man you don't care about rubbing your back, instead of doing it with the man you love, but in the end, you get to experience that love in your baby. It's beautiful. And I'm jealous."

"You'll have that someday, when the right woman comes along."

He exhales, his goofy smile leaving his face. "That's not my destiny. I'm not a one-woman kind of man. I'm a playboy. I'm a loyal soldier. I don't want my own empire. I don't want the fairy-tale. I want to die fighting for the people I love—and that won't be a woman who sleeps in my bed."

"Hey, I sleep in your bed."

He chuckles. "I meant, I won't die for a woman I fuck. I'll die protecting the Black empire. I'll die protecting Enzo, protecting you, protecting your baby. And I wouldn't have it any other way."

I swallow the lump in my throat as I look into his eyes. Langston loves me. Not in the same way Enzo does. But he loves me all the same. He would die for me. He would die for my baby.

I don't deserve his love. I could argue and say that's not what I want. That I don't want him to die like Zeke did. But that would dishonor the love he feels. So I don't tell him that.

I wrap my arms around him and say, "I love you too, Langston. But Liesel—"

"I can never love someone who can't love me back. Liesel doesn't love me."

I scrunch my face. "Are you sure? Because—"

"I'm sure. You don't know our history. There is nothing that could make her love me. Or me truly love her. You and Enzo come first."

———

I WRITE everything that Langston means to me. How much I love him. How thankful I am for all the times he helped me. All the times he protected me when he shouldn't have.

I feel the love flowing through me with each precious word.

I love you, Langston.

I'll never forget you, but I'm letting the pain go. Then I drop the letter into the water and watch it float away. And I hope one tiny piece of my heartbreak goes with it.

5

ENZO

LANGSTON ISN'T DEAD.

He's breathing.

The bullet grazed his arm.

He's alive.

I exhale all the breath I've been holding. But this fucker is about to die for almost killing Langston.

I dive on the man, forgetting I have a gun in my hand that could do just as good of a job. I pummel him to the ground, taking out all of my anger on this one man.

Langston sits, watching.

Finally, I stop. I aim the gun at the attacker's head.

"Where is Felix?" I ask.

The man shakes.

"Answer me, and I'll make your death quick. Keep the truth from me, and I'll torture you slowly."

The man glares at me. "Los Angeles. He's in Los Angeles."

I squeeze the trigger and watch him slump into the ground.

I don't know if the man was lying or telling the truth,

but it's the only lead I have to go on. So that's where I'll start.

Langston is still sitting, motionless. And I realize he can't do this. He can't chase Felix and my need for revenge all over the globe. He needs help, more than I can give him.

I need to get him help. But first, I need to destroy what is left of Felix's home.

"Come on," I grab Langston's hand, lifting him from the ground. He follows me silently.

I walk to the house and see where the charge wasn't connected to the explosives. I fix the mistake and then Langston and I head back to the car we rented and left on the edge of the property.

We turn around just before reaching the car, and I hold the button out to Langston, who presses it wordlessly.

The boom is enough to jolt us both back into reality. The building begins crumbling immediately, taking with it so many memories that will haunt me the rest of my days. I just hope this is the first step to healing.

I get Langston into the car, and we drive off, both of us staring into the rearview mirror watching the buildings crumble brick by brick.

I speed up when all we can see is the smoke floating high above the trees and buildings of the nearby town. The authorities will arrive soon, and I don't want to be near the wreckage when they arrive. Even though dealing with them would be no more than a little inconvenience.

I get us back to the yacht, and we leave Italy moments later. Langston still hasn't spoken to me, not one single word.

I know what I have to do next, but I just got him back, and I'm not ready to lose him again so soon. So I grip the ship's helm harder and stand, looking out at the endless ocean, hoping that in the time it takes me to get this yacht back to the states Langston will have made a miraculous recovery. Enough to be confident when we attack Felix, I won't have to worry about Langston dropping dead for real this time.

"It's okay," Langston says, while leaning against the doorframe.

I know what he means. It's okay I have to leave him on his own to heal. It's okay I'm abandoning him when he needs me the most. It's okay I need to go kill Felix instead of taking care of him.

But none of it feels okay. He is the only person left in the world I love. The only person I give a shit if they live or die.

And it breaks me that I have to leave him.

"Maybe—" I start.

"No."

I huff. "You didn't even let me tell you my plan." I don't have a good plan. Just that I could stay with him, go to a new city, get him settled, get him into therapy. Make sure he's healed, then we could attack Felix together.

"I don't need to hear your plan. You know it isn't a good plan anyway," he cracks a tiny smile at my expense.

"I have a great plan."

He shakes his head. "But it isn't the right plan. You need to kill Felix, now. It can't wait. Every day you wait is a day he corrupts more of our men. He gains more power. More money. More technology."

"It doesn't matter how long I wait. He took everything I love. There is nothing left he can take from me. Only you." Tears catch in the corner of my eye.

And I can see Langston's eyes watering. "Felix can't touch a dead man. He doesn't know I'm alive, so he can't come after me."

"I don't want to abandon you."

"You aren't. You are protecting me. You are avenging Kai and Liesel. You are protecting the motherfucking world."

I laugh. "I think that's a little dramatic. I don't think I'm protecting the whole world."

He shrugs with a cocky grin I haven't seen since he returned from the dead. "Maybe not the entire world, just our little part of it."

I nod. Because I can't speak. *Damn these tears and getting choked up all the time.*

"What do you want to do? Where are you going to go?" I ask finally, after clearing my throat a dozen times and wiping my tears on the back of my hand.

"I shouldn't tell you."

"Why not?"

"Because then I'll be safe to heal. Then you won't have to worry about me. You won't put your own life at risk to protect me. Felix can't torture you to get information about where I am because you don't know."

He's right, but I hate it.

"How will I find you when this is all over?"

He grins and raises his eyebrows. "I have faith you will be able to find me."

He's right. I have no problem tracking down someone who doesn't want to be found. It's one of my favorite activities, hunting down the hidden. I can find Langston, wherever he goes.

"Fine, don't tell me. Just promise me you will go see a therapist and get some help wherever you end up."

He nods.

Good enough.

"I think you should go to Hawaii, maybe Jamaica...no, Australia. That seems like your kind of place. Far away, warm. Filled with plenty of women in bikinis. You could learn to surf and spend your day teaching kids how to surf."

Langston just chuckles. "I don't have the patience for kids."

I laugh. "Maybe not."

I resist the urge to remind him if he truly wants to be lost, he needs to change his name. Stop using his bank account, credit cards, everything. He needs to exist only in the shadows. But I don't say anything, because he already knows all of that. We've grown up together. The three of us —Langston, Zeke, and I. We taught each other everything we know.

"Thanks for being the best brother I could have asked for," I say.

He pulls me into a hug. "Don't kid, we both know Zeke was the better brother."

I nod as we both start crying again. Zeke should be here. He should have survived. Instead, he's gone. And we are all that is left.

"Go kick your real brother's ass."

"Half-brother. And Felix, Milo, and Pietro may all be related to me by blood, but you and Zeke are my true brothers."

"I know."

Langston reaches into his pocket and pulls out a small item. He holds it in the palm of his hand.

"What's that?"

"You don't recognize it? I went to a lot of trouble to get it back."

I stare at the soot-covered item. It looks black more than silver, even though it's clear Langston tried to polish it at one point. Without a professional cleaning, it's black— which seems fitting.

I take the ring out of his hand. My mother's ring. The ring I gave Kai when I fake married her.

"Where did you get this?" I ask.

"Felix."

I'm speechless. Staring down at the soot-covered ring, I have so many feelings. This ring should still be on Kai's finger. I should have proposed for real. I should have married her.

Instead, it's just one more reminder of what I lost—one more momento to carry with me when I kill Felix. I take off the scrunchie I'm wearing and attach the ring to it.

It has part of Zeke, Kai, and now Langston. Pieces of all us now.

"Thank you."

"It's my fault Felix came back. I trusted him when I shouldn't have. Kill the bastard and fix my mistake."

It wasn't his mistake, but I know without therapy and time to heal, Langston won't feel differently. So I don't argue with him. I put the scrunchie back on my wrist.

"I will."

6

KAI

LIESEL IS A BITCH.

Delete, delete, delete...

Liesel is a whore.

No! Scratch out.

Why is it so hard for me to write a nice note about Liesel? She helped me—kept my secret. She was kind to me when she didn't have to be. But somehow every time I try to write a goodbye to her, it includes something mean.

Liesel loved Enzo—even with her dying breath. She would have tried to steal him back from me. I know that. And I think a part of me resents her for keeping Enzo from me for even a second. We had such a short time together. And a tiny reason Enzo and I had less time together was because of Liesel.

I hate her.

But the tears fall down from my eyes onto the page, and it's obvious I'm telling myself a lie.

I love her.

She was my only female friend. The only one who

understood why I wanted to hide this pregnancy—*the only one.*

And as much as I didn't get my happily ever after, she didn't either. And that kills me. She deserved to live a long, happy life. She deserved to have time to decide if she wanted to find her child she gave up to protect. She deserved more time, and now she's gone.

I drop my pen. I can't write anymore. These notes were a stupid idea. I can't let go of people I love. I can't let go of the pain. I can't let go of any of it.

I rip off the note I started writing for Liesel and let the pieces fall into the river. Then I rip another piece from the notebook and do the same with that one.

This actually feels good. So I rip another and another as more tears fall, anger spreads, and pain consumes me.

"You know that's littering," Beckett says.

I keep ripping the last page of the notebook. "So fine me. But the world owes me. I think I deserve a moment to litter if it makes me feel better."

"I'm not judging," Beckett says, leaning over the railing of the bridge next to me.

I don't want him to see me cry. I don't know how much he knows about my past. I don't know what my father has told him. But I still have my suspicions about him. I don't think he's just a fisherman, even though he looks the part. He's wearing cargo pants and a flannel shirt. And he does smell like fish.

"You smell," I say, wiping the tears from my eyes. He probably thinks I'm crying because of pregnancy hormones.

"We live in Alaska; everyone smells like fish."

I sigh.

"Want to tell me what the ripping up the tiny pieces of paper was about?"

"Nope."

He nods. "Want to go get a coffee with me?"

"I can't drink caffeine; it could hurt the baby."

"Oh." He stares at my huge stomach. I'm only a little over half-way through the pregnancy, but I can't imagine my stomach growing any more than it already has. "Well, not too much longer, and then you'll be able to have caffeine again once the baby is born."

I frown. "When do you think the baby is due?"

"A week or two?"

I laugh. "I look that big, huh? I'm just over half-way through. I still have months left."

His eyes bulge in his head. "Really? I don't think your stomach has any more room to grow."

"Well, that's a helpful comment," I growl snakily.

He laughs. "Sorry, I don't know what to say around pregnant women."

"But you do know how to talk around people, right?"

He nods, laughing harder now. "You have a lot of spunk. You are a lot like your father; you know that?"

I shake my head and turn back to the water. "I wouldn't know."

"What do you mean?"

"He isn't really my father."

"Oh," Beckett says, staring out at the water. Neither of us speaks for a moment, just soaking up the beauty that is Alaska.

"Let's go get something to eat," he eventually says.

"Why?"

"So I can tell you you are wrong."

"About what?"

"Who your father is."

He starts walking then, not waiting for me to follow. He knows I will; I'm too intrigued.

There is a small cafe that serves mainly seafood. A smell I'm getting more averse to the bigger my stomach grows. We both sit at a small table outside overlooking the creek.

Beckett orders a salad with salmon.

And I order a grilled cheese.

"Really? A grilled cheese?" he asks.

"Yes, I'm sick of seafood."

He grins. "You're just like your father. He took up the job of fisherman. He used to work on yachts for a living, but he hates fish."

"That's your big reason why I'm like my father? Because we both hate fish?"

"No, that's not why." He leans back in his chair and studies me. "Do you know who I am?"

"You're Beckett," I say, not offering that I think he's security my father hired to help protect me. And that my father also tried to set the two of us up on a date because he's close to my age.

He nods. "What else?"

"You're a smug asshole, who thinks he knows more about my life than I do because you spent some time with my uncle."

He leans forward with a smug smile. "I am those things. But I'm also right. Because I spent months alone with your father. And there wasn't a single day that passed when he didn't talk about you."

He leans back.

I swallow down the lump. It doesn't mean anything. My uncle-father fucked up so many times. I've moved past what he did. I'll even call him father. But that doesn't mean he really is.

"Who am I?" he asks again, with a challenging raised eyebrow.

"Beckett—a dickhead."

"Who am I?"

"A douchebag."

"Who am I?"

"A dumbass."

"Who am I?"

"You're my security guard! Okay...you're my security guard, bodyguard, whatever you want to call it. You're here to protect and take care of me, happy?"

He smiles, smugly. "Yes, I am. Your father hired me initially to track you down and make sure you were safe. He hired me to pull you out of that situation before the final round, because even after everything he did to prepare you —even after making sure there was no way the boy couldn't fall in love with you, couldn't kill you, he still wouldn't put your fate in Enzo's hands. He hired me to pull you out of there and keep you safe."

"My uncle doesn't have anything to do with Enzo falling in love with me."

"Yes, he does. Enzo loves playing the knight in shining armor, the rescuer, even if he will never admit it. Your father made sure you were in need of rescuing."

I frown.

"And your father made sure you didn't die. He sent me to keep that from happening. I pulled you out of that car before you caught on fire. I saved you, because your father sent me to."

"That doesn't mean he's my father."

"Sure, it does."

"You really saved me? You were the one that pulled me to safety?"

He nods.

Our food is delivered. And we eat in silence. When I finish my last bite, he reaches into his pocket and pulls out a key.

"What's this?"

"A key to your house."

"My house? I don't have enough money to own a house."

He laughs. "Sure, you do. Why do you think your father has been saving all his money for years? Why did he make you live in a trailer park instead of a house? So when you really needed the money to disappear, to live off of instead of being vulnerable to the Black organization, you would have it."

My eyes grow big as I pick up the key. "Come on, I'll show you. I thought it might be better if he showed you. But you're stubborn. You need to be convinced of how good your father really is. And your father will never say he's a good father."

I frown. "You do realize he sold me, right? He had me beaten every day for years."

He hesitates. "I know that sometimes as parents, we make the wrong choices for our kids—terrible choices. Choices that at the time, we see as the only way out. But that doesn't mean he is any less your father. Or that he loves you any less."

I feel my heart opening to my father again. Even opening to being a little friendlier toward Beckett. He's being nice, even if my father is paying him to be nice.

Beckett drives me in his Jeep. He blasts country music the entire time.

"I didn't know you were from the south?"

"I'm not, but my ex was. She got me into country music."

That's when I realize Beckett is also dealing with a broken heart.

He slows the car at the end of a gravel road about two minutes from my father's house. But unlike that one-bedroom cabin, this is a house. A real house—no, a mansion.

"Oh, my god," I say as my jaw drops at the sight of it. "There is no way I can afford this house."

"It's already paid for."

"Wow," I step out of the car and slam the door shut. It's a two-story cabin, with giant windows at the front. It backs up to the edge of a hillside, and I can't wait to see the view from the back.

I start walking to the door.

"You are so cute when you waddle," Beckett says.

"I do not waddle," I say, although I totally do.

He chuckles. "Come on." He holds the door open for me, and I step inside.

The entrance is amazing. It's double-height, and you can see straight through the house to the incredible view at the back.

I walk through the ginormous kitchen; seriously, it's huge. I don't know what I will do with all the cabinet space. I spot the stone fireplace I'm already in love with in the corner of the living room. And then I walk outside onto the deck that could easily hold fifty people. I was right; it has a view of a canyon full of evergreens and a private lake. The view is breathtaking.

"The house has four bedrooms, three baths, a jacuzzi, and this view. And you're telling me the man who did all of this isn't your father?"

Tears, damn tears. *My father did all of this for me. He ensured I lived, no matter the cost.*

"He even started on a nursery, but then figured you would want to be able to decorate it yourself."

For the first time, despite the pain, I can see a future. One that isn't just bleak. One that isn't just dripping in pain. One where I can learn to live again.

My father is in my life again. And I decide here and now to give him a fresh start. Whatever his past mistakes, he loves me now. And I need people that love me.

And despite Beckett being hired by my father, he could become a good friend too. Nothing more—we would never be lovers. Never fall in love. But we could be friends.

This is my life now. And for the first time, I feel like I'm finally letting go of my past. I'm finally facing my future.

And then I feel the pain in my stomach. It rips through my body like fire. Shuttering any promise that the future is going to be bright. I grip my stomach as I fall to the floor in pain.

This can't be happening. The baby has to be okay. Because as much as I'm letting go, I can't let go of the only piece I have left of Enzo.

7

ENZO

I DROPPED Langston off in Miami, before taking a flight to Los Angeles. By now he has already disappeared. If I return to Miami, I won't find him. And I don't know if that comforts me or rips my heart out more.

This isn't goodbye. It's just temporary. He's alive, but for now, he has to remain dead.

Now, I'm in LA. And I have no idea if this is a dead-end or not. *What would Felix be doing in LA? Is he hiding? Regrouping?* If he is trying to get control of my technology, money, and team, then he is in the wrong place. Miami is where he needs to be.

This is definitely a dead end. I should do my own research to find Felix. But Langston was always the best at hunting people down, digging into their pasts.

I'm on my own.

I head into the first bar I see, knowing if anyone is going to know about criminal activity in this city, it's going to be in a bar. But more importantly, I need a drink.

I hate sitting at the bar. I feel exposed; you have to make small talk with the bartender and the other people sitting at the bar. But it's the best place to find out any information about whether or not Felix is here. Sitting at the goddamn bar.

There is only one person sitting at the bar, though—a blonde woman in a tight red dress.

Holy shit!

It can't be...

I'm dreaming. I have to be. Even if Liesel is alive, the chances of me seeing her while walking into the first bar I see in one of the biggest cities in the country is astronomical. The odds are not in my favor. I'm definitely dreaming.

But the woman turns as if sensing something important is happening behind her.

Our eyes connect.

Then our hearts.

This is real.

She stands, dropping her glass of chardonnay on the floor as we run into each other's arms.

"You're alive," we both say at the same time as my arms wrap around her tiny frame, and she buries her tear-streaked face in my chest.

I hold her tightly, as another piece of my heart heals. Another part of me is whole again.

"How?" we both ask.

But the tears tell me it's the wrong question.

"Kai?" I ask.

Her jaw tightens, and more tears fall as she slowly shakes her head no.

Langston and now Liesel have both confirmed they think Kai is dead. Felix said she was dead, but I don't believe a word out of his mouth. I saw the evidence myself. But somehow the ghosts of my life keep finding a way back to me.

Langston.

Liesel.

They both died.

But yet, here is Liesel.

"Langston's alive too," I say.

She bites her lip like she wants to say something but decides against it. Finally, she says, "Is he here?"

"No, he um..." I rub my neck. *How do I tell her he had a psychotic break?* "He decided he needed to stay dead a little longer."

She nods. "Let's get a drink."

We both sit at the bar. She orders another chardonnay. I order a whiskey.

"What are you doing in LA?" I ask.

She stiffens, her fingers sliding up and down the stem of her wine glass. "It doesn't matter."

"Liesel? Are you in trouble?"

She shakes her head. "Not anymore. I was broken. Devastated by all that I had lost. I needed to get away. I needed to find something worth living for again. This is where I ended up."

I can read between the lines. I know what she isn't saying. She came here to find the child she gave up, the only thing in her head worth living for. But if she doesn't want to talk about it, I won't ask.

"You should know, Felix is possibly here, in LA," I say.

Her shoulders tense at Felix's name.

"Are you sure?"

"I don't know yet. I'm following a lead. It could be nothing, or he could be here."

She nods. "I shouldn't be here. I shouldn't be talking to you."

I hate how all the people I love have to run from me to

stay safe. Danger follows me everywhere. She's right. She isn't safe with me.

I wish Langston had come with me. I could have told him to take Liesel with him. Protect her and keep her safe. They both love each other. But he's already gone. And I have no way to contact him.

I could suspend my search for Felix, find Langston instead, get Liesel somewhere safe, then resume my hunt for Felix again.

"You have to disappear. You have to remain dead. If Felix thinks you are dead, then you are in no danger."

She nods.

"Do you know how to do that? Disappear?"

She bites her lip covered in red lipstick. "Yes—no. I don't know."

"Give me your purse."

She hands it to me.

I pull out her credit cards, her driver's license, and any other identifying pieces of information. I put them all in my pocket. I will incinerate them as soon as I leave here.

I pull out all the cash I have and shove it into her purse.

Her eyes widen.

"You will never use credit cards again. You will not return to your apartment. You will not use your name again. Not until Langston or I find you and tell you it is safe, understand?"

She nods, but I can see the fear.

"You can do this. There are thousands of dollars of cash in there. You only have to stay hidden until Felix is dead. Then you will be safe. A couple of weeks tops."

She nods.

"Let me get you an ID," I say.

"ID?"

"Yes, if you decide to buy a plane ticket you will need one. If you need a job, find an hourly one, preferably a wait-ressing job or something that pays mostly in tips. That way, you don't need a social security number. Don't stay in one place for long. Don't go anywhere you've ever lived before. Don't stay with any family or friends."

She frowns at that one. I know she doesn't have any family or friends outside of Langston and me.

I spot a group of girls in the corner bar. Two out of the five are blonde, and Liesel could pass for either.

"Wait here, I'll be right back," I say.

I wipe the makeup from my shirt where Liesel hugged me, and then I strut over to the women. I wish Kai was here; she's always better at stealing things than I am.

"Ladies!" I say, holding my arms out and ensuring my shirt rises enough to see my hard abs. "Can I buy you all a round of shots?"

All the women ogle my body.

"Aren't you with that woman over there?" one of the women says—most likely the smart, reasonable, not currently drunk one.

"She's my sister. She likes to play wingman sometimes," I say with a wink, slurring just enough of my words that my next move is believable.

"Sure, we want tequila shots!" one of the women says.

"Tequila it is then!" I stumble, landing in the blonde woman on the end's lap. She grins, not at all upset that I fell on top of her.

"It looks like someone had too much to drink. You should come home with me," she says, stroking my chest.

I grin wider, as I reach into her purse and pull out her wallet. I then shove it into my back pocket.

"Maybe," I wiggle my eyebrows. "First, those shots." I

stumble up and back to the bar next to Liesel. I flag the bartender to start on the shots, and then I slide the wallet into Liesel's purse.

"Smooth," she says with a smile.

"You understand all the rules? You disappear. Keep a low profile. Don't talk on the phone. Don't surf the internet. Nothing. Understood?"

"Yes."

"Last thing," I reach into her purse and pull out her cell phone. This will be the hardest part for Liesel. "You can't use your cell phone. Ideally, no phones at all. But if you absolutely need one, then use a payphone or buy a burner phone. Understand? Don't borrow someone else's. Don't trust anyone, but me and Langston."

She nods, then leans over and kisses me on the cheek. "Don't worry. I'm good at playing dead."

Liesel gets up and walks out of the bar—out of my life.

Two dead people have returned to my life. Two ghosts have reappeared only to disappear again.

My heart clenches—*Kai.*

Could she be alive too?

Whether she is alive or not, it makes no difference. My mission is the same. Kill Felix. Take out anyone who followed him over me. Ensure that if Kai is alive, she is safe.

8

KAI

"You're going to be fine," Beckett says as he drives me down the hill to the small clinic. This town doesn't even have a hospital. I have no idea how close the nearest hospital is, but I'm guessing close to an hour plane or boat ride away.

My head feels dizzy, I want to vomit, and I feel the blood trickling between my legs.

Please, God, don't let this baby die.

"You're going to be fine," Beckett repeats.

"I don't care about me! I'm worried about the baby."

"Well, if you die, the baby dies, so you better care about living."

I growl. "Just drive."

He sighs. "Take my hand."

"What? Why?"

"Just trust me. It will make you feel better."

I glare. *Was he listening to anything I was saying?*

"It will help calm you down, which will lower your anxiety and blood pressure, which will help the baby."

I grab his hand quickly and forcibly. I squeeze his hand

with everything I have, partially from being angry with him, and partially from being so scared about what I'm facing.

"The baby is going to be fine," he says.

"You don't know that," I say, my voice shaky.

"Yes, I do."

I shake my head. "Everything that can go wrong goes horribly in my life."

He frowns. "Just focus on my hand. I need you to squeeze as hard as you possibly can. Focus on that, nothing else."

I look down at where I'm already gripping his hand tightly. I squeeze harder, watching as his hand turns from red to white.

"Just like that, Kai."

I take a deep breath, the nerves easing just a little.

"Tell me about him," he says.

I freeze. "Who?"

He chuckles. "Enzo, the love of your life. Tell me what he'd be doing if he were here, and I'll do it. Even if it means kissing you." He winks as he says the last sentence, and I can't help but smile just a little.

"He'd be a wreck, but he wouldn't let me know. He'd be calm, all business. He'd have me hold his hand like you are doing. He'd talk to me and distract me. Maybe ask me what names we should call the baby. He thinks it's a boy. I think it's a girl."

"Oh, yea? Well, what names do you have in mind?"

"Honestly, I haven't thought about it much." Mainly because I can't imagine naming my child without Enzo. And there are too many dead people I should honor to include them all in the child's name.

"How about Jamie?"

"No."

"Beatrice?"

"No."

"Greta?"

"No," I laugh. "You are horrible at this."

His eyes go to the door of the clinic. Apparently, he is not horrible at distracting me, though, because we are here. He jumps out of the car and has my door open and my hand in his again as he helps me out of the car. I lean on him as we walk to the check-in at the clinic.

"I called twenty-minutes ago to let you know Katherine was coming in," he says.

"If you will just have a seat—"

"No, we will not be having a seat. We would like to see a doctor, now," Beckett says. He towers over her, giving her a look that says *either you show us to an exam room right now or I will burst through the wall myself.*

It works.

The woman nods and leads us through a hallway to exam room three. There are only three exam rooms in this entire clinic I realize.

Beckett helps me ease into a chair, before kneeling next to me still holding my hand.

I'm covered in sweat, I feel like I'm burning up, I'm light-headed, and my stomach feels heavy like a thousand pounds of brick are weighing me down.

"How was I? Did I measure up to Enzo?" he asks.

"Yes," I nod.

"Good, now what would he do?"

"He would give them sixty-seconds to get a doctor in here before he would open the door and drag the nearest doctor inside against their will and threaten their lives if they don't treat me immediately."

Beckett looks at his watch. "Sixty-seconds starts now."

I purse my lips as I exhale. I'm still holding Beckett's hand. I can't believe I ever doubted him. He's a good man. I get the same feelings as when I held Zeke or Langston's hand. But nothing more.

In some ways, I wish I would get even the tiniest bit of tingle in my fingers touching his hand. Some sort of spark. Anything. Not because I want to start dating right now, I don't. I'm not over Enzo. I will never be over Enzo. But just to know I could rebuild my life with someone would give me hope.

"What?" he asks.

"Nothing," I say, still staring at our hands.

"Time's up," he says.

Just as he gets up to hunt down the doctor, the door opens. And my father stands in the doorway.

I immediately burst into tears at the sight of him standing there with worry marrying his face.

"I'm grabbing a doctor. Hold her hand," Beckett says, tag-teaming with my father before he races out the door. My father takes my hand.

"You haven't seen the doctor yet?" he asks.

I shake my head, trying to keep the tears at bay.

He grabs my head and pulls me to his chest. "You don't have to be strong anymore. Let it all out. And I'm going to kill the doctor myself if he lets anything happen to you."

The door opens again, and Beckett is shoving the doctor through the door, eyes glaring at the back of his head. He's doing a good job trying to do what Enzo would do in this situation. The main difference would be Enzo would already have a gun pointed at the doctor's head.

But even though he's doing everything he can to be Enzo, he's not Enzo. No one can replace him.

"Hello, Miss Katherine, I'm—"

"Does it look like she needs introductions? She's in pain and scared, just help her."

The doctor gives Beckett a dirty look.

"Can you tell me how you are feeling?" the doctor asks me as Beckett resumes his position by my side. Between my father on one side and Beckett on the other, it's hard for the doctor to get close to me.

"I feel lightheaded, I passed our earlier, I feel like I might vomit, my stomach feels hard as a rock, and I'm bleeding pretty heavily."

"Hmm, I see," the doctor says.

"You see? What the hell does it mean?" this time, my father is the one to chastise the doctor.

The doctor ignores the question. "I'm going to listen to your heart and take your blood pressure."

The doctor does his best to finagle around the two men standing guard over me while he runs the simple tests. "Your pulse and blood pressure are both high."

"What does that mean?" all three of us say at the same time.

"Not sure yet. Have you been feeling any anxiety lately?"

"Yes, but only after my symptoms started."

He nods. "I would like to run a few more tests. Get some blood work down, a urine test, and an ultrasound will give us the best idea of what is happening with the baby."

"Great, let's do the ultrasound first," I say.

"I'll have the front desk call to send for the ultrasound technician. But first the blood and urine."

I agree.

And both men hold my hand through the blood draw even though I'm not in pain from the needle stick, just the unknown future of my baby.

The men both reluctantly leave me alone in the bathroom for the urine test, but as soon as I exit the bathroom, both are at my side again as we wait for the doctor to return to do the ultrasound.

The doctor enters a few seconds later, not wanting Beckett to come hunt him down again.

"Okay, it looks like it will take about an hour, possibly an hour and a half for the technician to get here. In the meantime, we have a small room with a bed you should rest and try to relax in while we wait for the technician and results."

"An hour? Are you fucking kidding me?" my father says.

"You know how it works here. We live in a small town, and it's going to take that long for our technician to catch a flight over. Your only other option is to pay for a medical flight for Katherine from here to the nearest hospital. But that could take twice as long, will be very expensive, and at this point, I don't think it's necessary. I believe she is just experiencing some anxiety and high blood pressure. Rest should do the trick."

Beckett gives my hand a tight squeeze before he releases it and walks over into the doctor's space. "Do you know how to work the ultrasound machine?"

"In theory. It's been years since I've done an ultrasound."

"Well, you are about to get some on the job experience," Beckett says.

The doctor stares at all of us, none of us willing to back down. He sighs. "I'll get the machine set up and see if it gives us any insight."

The seconds tick by as I lay back on the exam table with the two men flanking either side of me.

The doctor takes his sweet time setting up the machine, fumbling with buttons, and then squirting the gooey ooze onto my stomach. He places the wand on my stomach and begins moving it around.

The screen isn't facing me, so I have no idea what the doctor sees on the screen or if he sees anything.

Hours tick by. In reality, it was only a few minutes, but in my head, worry has paused time. I can't speak, my voice is gone, my heart is beating frantically with hope that the baby is still okay. That my little part of Enzo isn't gone.

I look into my father's eyes. Tears are now free-falling down his face, his nose is red, and his face solemn. He's already given up hope that the baby is still alive. But the fact that it affects him this much surprises me and makes my heart forgive him that tiny amount I was never going to give him. I was never going to fully forgive him. I do now.

I look to my left where Beckett is gripping my hand like if he lets go, I'll fall to my death. I may not physically fall, but without the strength of these two men holding onto me, I would fall. I would die. I've felt heartbreak before. I live with heartbreak every single day. This baby is the only thing keeping me alive. Without the baby, I'd be dead, from a broken heart.

My heart thuds louder in my chest, each beat potentially being my last. With one word from the doctor telling me the baby is gone, my heart will shatter again. My heart is already weak and vulnerable. This time it wouldn't be a slow sputtering into darkness. This time I will rapidly decline until my last breath.

I will have nothing left to fight for. And the pain of losing Enzo combined with the pain of losing my child is too much.

"Doctor?" Beckett asks, blinking back tears as he looks into the doctor's terrified face.

I tighten my grip on both men's hands. Preparing as best as I can for the coming words. Words that will do more damage than any knife or bullet ever could. His words will pierce right through my heart—healing it or obliterating it.

The doctor looks at Beckett, then at my father. Silently saying something with just his glance.

No, no, no, no...

The only reason he would have to prepare them is if the news is bad. And I can't handle it.

The doctor finally looks at me. I can't read his face. His expression has changed. His words slow. And then he delivers the news that will change my life forever...

9

ENZO

I FOUND Felix two days ago.

It took everything in me not to shoot him dead in the street the first time I saw him climbing into his Lamborghini. But I need information before I can kill him. I need to know every person who backs him. I need to know every person following him. Every person responsible for Kai's death. Because none of them get to survive. And I want no one left to continue the Black organization. The ones on my side need to find new jobs. And the ones against me deserve to die slowly and tortuously.

So I've been tracking Felix's movements from the shadows. And he's in Los Angeles to gather more men. To get more people on his side. He's not trying to expand the Black organization to make more money. He's gathering men because he thinks I'm going to attack, and he needs more men to defeat me.

I should take it as a compliment.

But I just want this to end. I'm tired of fighting. And every man Felix gathers is one more man I have to kill.

So on the second night, I've seen enough. Felix can't live. I can't slowly torture him for months. He needs to die tonight.

Liesel deserves to walk without looking over her shoulder worried that Felix will reappear.

Langston deserves to heal without thinking he is only healing to take Felix down.

And Kai deserves for her killer to be slain.

Tonight is the night Felix Black dies. The night I kill the last of my half-brothers. And tomorrow I go to work wiping out any of his remaining followers. The day after that, I end the Black organization for good. And then I spend the rest of my life protecting Liesel and Langston from suffering any more pain. That's the least I can do.

Felix sticks to his routine from the other night. At six, he leaves his hotel, chosen because it's more secure compound than hotel due to the number of people he has surrounding and protecting him at all areas of the property. It's not enough. He may feel safe with dozens of men, but they are a mere inconvenience for me to get through. He may think he's protected with the best security systems, but the technology is just one more thing for me to dismantle and show him exactly how vulnerable he is. He may think his weapons will keep him safe, his threat of retaliation with explosives too great for me to mess with, but it's simply another weakness I plan on exploiting.

I have nothing to fear anymore.

Felix still thinks Langston and Liesel are dead.

And Kai really is dead.

He can't hurt me. I'm invincible when I have nothing to fear.

My blood boils when I see Felix walk into a club notorious for selling women. The club also sells weapons, drugs, and anything else the owner thinks will make him money, women being his highest seller. He attracts the wealthiest men in the world, because he has the cops in his pocket and guarantees to have the most attractive women for the men to buy.

It makes me sick.

I guess I'm bringing down more than one man tonight.

The club should be impossible for me to get in, but growing up with one of the biggest criminals in the world as your father gives you some advantages. My father had hundreds of illegal clubs. I know how security at these places works.

So I buy an expensive suit, rent the most expensive car I can find, and then drive up to the front door of the place and step out like I own the entire world. A place like this doesn't have exits. There is only one entrance and one exit. At least known exits.

There is always a hidden exit to get their most exclusive clientele out fast if need be, but that would take days of research to find and exploit. I don't want to wait days. Not to mention dealing with the security cameras and the armed guards. The best way in is the easiest.

I walk up to the man who serves as security for the club, deciding who goes to the floor of the club, the part that keeps things legal and is the front for the business. Versus the basement, where the real money exchanges hands. That's where Felix is. That is where I want to go.

"Name?" the man says, but his eyes slowly widen when he takes in my attire and expensive car. He knows exactly which room to take me to, but he doesn't know my name. His sole job is to know my name, to know who I am, and to make me feel like royalty when I walk in so I'll come back again and again.

"I'm so sorry, Mr..." the man says, waiting for me to fill in the blank.

I could lie. I could say any name in the world, and he would accept it. He doesn't care what my name is. I'm sure half the men that come here lie about their names.

But I don't want to do this as someone else. I want to kill as the monster I am.

"I'm Enzo Black."

The man's mouth falls, his face whitens, and his shoulders tense. "I'm so sorry, Mr. Black. Right this way, sir," the man in the suit says as he stumbles forward like he made the biggest mistake of his life, and he's about to get slaughtered for it.

I don't doubt that if I were to tell Mr. Sullivan, the owner of the club, of this man's mistake that he would be. My name is notorious in the underground. Even on the other side of the country. I can go into any club like this I want. And pay half as anyone else to get the same drugs, weapons, or women, because no one wants to piss me off.

The man leads me down a long hallway. I see the sweat dripping down his neck, his anxiety palpable. He has nothing to worry about, though. I'm not going to rat him out. I have much bigger fish to fry.

He opens the door for me, and I step into the room, hazy with the smoke of expensive cigars.

Silence slowly falls around the room as each man recognizes who I am. One by one eyes widen then change—to anger, to fear, to loyalty. Each man in this room is powerful. Each man in this room runs a criminal empire. But none of them match the power I have. Half of them's livelihood depends on me to supply them weapons or technology to keep them safe. The other half have been attacked as my enemy in the past.

And only one man seems to enjoy that I'm here—Felix.

"Mr. Black," the man who showed me to the room says, introducing me to the room, as if I need an introduction.

Felix scowls as the man says my name. He wants the title. He wants to be the sole Mr. Black.

Not going to happen. I'm going to destroy the Black name.

"Gentleman," I say with a cocky smirk.

Sullivan stands from his chair, suddenly more nervous by my presence. This is the type of club that doesn't screen for weapons. They know the only way any high powered man would step into a club like this is with protection. Every man in here has a weapon. They have bodyguards lining the walls.

But there are only two men in this room who know how to wield a weapon—Felix and me. We are the only two men in the room who could not only start a war but finish it.

Felix is here to gain Mr. Sullivan's loyalty. He won't be starting a war.

But Sullivan has no idea why I'm here. And that scares him. It should because starting a war is the least of what I'll do.

"We are just about to start the entertainment for tonight. You can have my seat here." Sullivan leads me to his chair like I'm incapable of finding it by myself. And then snaps his fingers.

A woman wearing nothing but panties and six-inch heels struts in. "What can I get you to drink, honey?" she asks.

"Scotch," I say, my blood already boiling.

But I keep my anger from showing.

The woman returns promptly with my drink as the

"entertainment" starts. And by entertainment, I mean torture.

Two hours later, I'm sick. I literally feel like I'm going to vomit. The amount of women these men are buying does something to my insides. Acid is burning from the inside out.

My plan was to wait until the end, then do my damage. But I can't wait any longer.

I pull out my cell phone and press the button that will bring the second man down tonight, and then I wait. It takes five fucking more minutes before I hear the sirens in the distance grow close.

Sullivan looks at me, and he immediately knows what I've done. He pays off the police chief to ignore what he does. Of course, the police chief just thinks he runs an illegal gambling ring for high rollers. He has no idea the criminal things that actually happen. Until now.

Sullivan thought he was safe from the police. But I have more money and power than he ever will. The police aren't going to be able to get every man here. But if they capture one, it will be enough to ruin Sullivan's reputation. It will be enough to take this club down.

I wait, knowing this place is about to erupt, and it will be the perfect time to make my move.

Seconds later, Sullivan loses his cool, knowing I just cost him everything.

He pulls out his gun, but I fire faster. I don't kill him, that would be too easy for this bastard. But I hit him hard enough in the core to do serious damage to his liver.

Chaos erupts. Men start firing in every direction as they scramble to get out the secret exit at the back reserved for this exact situation. None of the men know who is the enemy or their ally. So they attack everyone as their foe.

I spot Felix trying to move through the crowd of men out the exit.

I follow, moving quickly toward my single mission. I press the gun to the base of his head.

"Leaving already? We haven't even had a chance to talk privately yet," I say.

He chuckles. "I don't think this is the place to have a private conversation."

"Really? With all the terrified women getting in the way and guns firing?"

"What do you want, Enzo?"

"I want you dead."

He laughs. "You won't kill me."

I press the gun harder as I walk him out the back door and into an alleyway. There were too many stray bullets flying in the club. I don't want to chance a stray bullet being what ends Felix's life. I want to be the one to do it.

When we are alone, I hit him in the face as hard as I can with the end of the gun. Blood spews from his mouth.

"Was that really necessary?" he asks, spitting more blood.

"I don't get to torture you slowly, as was my original plan. So I'm going to make you suffer as much as I can tonight."

He shakes his head with a devious grin. "You won't kill me tonight."

"Yes, I will."

"You would have already killed me if you were going to tonight. You might be the death of me one day, Enzo. I don't doubt that. I have respect for you enough to remember you were the one who killed both of my brothers. You killed our father. That's all you do—kill. Most likely, I will die at your hands. But not tonight."

I press the gun against his temple. He holds his hands up with a chuckle when I don't immediately pull the trigger.

What the hell is stopping me?

I don't care that he's my brother. I think at one point that stopped me, but not anymore. *What's stopping me from pulling the trigger now?*

"Hope," he says.

I still. "What?"

"You have hope. Hope that your friends survived. Hope that I have answers. Hope that Kai is alive."

He's right; I do have hope. I was wrong about Langston. Wrong about Liesel. *Am I wrong about Kai too?*

I grab his throat as I pocket my gun. This is personal. He will die at my hands, but not my weapon.

"What do you know?" I ask as I strangle his throat with my hands.

His face brightens. He's won. He knows it. This is who Felix is. A snake that plays games with my head. I should know by now not to trust him.

Which is why when he said Kai was dead, I needed to see for myself. The same with Langston and Liesel. The evidence was there, pointing to their demises. But I was wrong about Langston and Liesel.

"What are you asking, Enzo?" Felix asks, so fucking calm even though I literally hold his life in my hands.

We've fought before. We are an equal match. But right now, I have the upper hand. Right now, with the anger and pain flowing through me, there is nothing that could stop me from killing him if I wanted to.

"Did you lie?"

Felix's lips curl into an evil grin. "I lie about a lot of things Enzo. Which lie are you referring to?"

I can't believe I'm going to say these words. I know the

evidence. And I can't trust Felix. If I want to search for myself to see if Kai is alive, I need to do it. But not because of anything Felix says. I won't ask. I don't need to hear more lies from Felix.

Just kill him.

Felix sees the fight within me. He sees the turmoil and of course, he takes advantage.

"Kai is alive," he says.

My heart stops.

My world stops.

Everything stops.

I'm good at reading people. Good at determining when they are telling the truth or a lie. But with Felix, it's impossible to tell. He only shows what he wants you to see.

And right now, I know this is about survival for him. He's giving me hope that he is the only person in the world who will be able to find Kai. He knows that will keep him alive.

Kill him.

I squeeze tighter around his neck so that he can't breathe.

But he's calm. Too calm. He raises an eyebrow as if to say, *why am I still alive if you want me dead?*

Because he fucking gave me hope. He dangled the one thing I want more than anything in the world in front of me. And now I don't know what to do with that.

"Where is she?" I ask, showing no restraint—playing all of my cards at once.

Felix laughs. "Safe. Alive. And mine."

I shove him hard against the brick wall behind him. "Where. Is. She?"

"Safe, with the man I planted in her life. She has no idea he's the enemy. No idea the man she's falling in love with is also the man who will snuff out her life with one phone call from me."

"Liar." I slam him against the wall harder. There is no way Kai is falling in love with another man. Not so soon. Not while still pregnant. Not possible.

"Pull out my phone," Felix says, taunting me.

Don't listen to him. He's a liar.

But my hope that Kai is alive overrules any common sense I have when it comes to Felix.

I release him, pull out my gun, and aim it at his head again as I reach into his pocket and pull out his cell phone.

"Look at the text messages from Beckett," he says.

I open his text messages. And find the messages. Hundreds of messages. All pictures of Kai.

These could be fake. He could have manipulated old photos of Kai to make it look like she's still alive somewhere else.

But it doesn't stop my heart from speeding rapidly at the thought that Kai is alive.

She's alive.

For the first time in weeks, I have hope. I have a reason to live that doesn't involve killing other people.

"How?" I ask.

"If that is the question you are asking, it's, as usual, the wrong one. Kai is strong, fearless, and unstoppable. Do you really think she was going to let me kill her with a little explosion? She fought harder for her life, for her child's life."

I frown.

"You should have had more faith in her than that. The fact that you believed she was dead so easily is ridiculous."

He's right. I should have fought harder for her. I should have searched the end of the earth for her.

I scroll through more pictures of her. Still not fully believing that she is alive, even though I have pictures in my hand. Felix is a liar. This could all be a lie, to torture me with.

But then I see the clearest image out of the bunch. Most of the pictures are blurry or half shots of her taken quickly so that she won't notice that a picture is being taken. But the last image is the clearest.

It's a full-on shot of Kai, her belly has doubled in size since the last time I saw her, there is a fresh pain in her eyes, and there is another man with his hand on her shoulder.

I told Kai when she ran, to really run. To not look back. That I would find her. And she hid in the last place I or anyone else would ever look for her.

But it wasn't enough, Felix found her. And now I have too.

I will keep her safe.

"So you see, you won't kill me," Felix says.

I growl. "You underestimate my need to keep Kai safe."

He shakes his head. "That's exactly why you won't kill me."

"What did you do?"

"I tied my life to hers."

I hold up his cell phone. "But I have the key to ensuring your man doesn't kill Kai before I get there. He texts you regularly, and you respond. All I have to do is keep up the charade until I've reached Alaska and killed him."

He smirks. "So you've figured out where Kai is. Good for you. I always knew you were the smart one in the family," he says sarcastically.

"You should choose your last words more carefully."

"The text exchange isn't what is keeping Kai alive."

I frown.

"What then?"

"Kill me and find out."

He won't tell me. He could be bluffing. This whole thing could be an elaborate lie. But my hope is too strong.

And my fear of losing Kai stronger.

I won't risk her life to get my revenge.

I growl and then knock him out with my gun.

Felix is right—I can't kill him. Not until I figure out how his life is tied to Kai. *Is Beckett the only man who will be ready to kill her if Felix is reported dead? Are there others? Did he hook up some explosives? What?*

I don't know.

I just know I need Felix contained until I can figure out if Kai is alive. And how to keep her safe.

I pull out my own cell and dial the direct line to detective Perry.

"Hello?" he answers.

"I have another one for you. In the back alley behind the club. He was trying to make an escape, but I knocked him out."

"Good work, I'll be right there."

I hang up as I wait for the police to apprehend Felix. It's a temporary solution at best. Felix will escape prison easily. He has too much money and resources not to. But it will give me a head start.

Felix starts coming to as the footsteps approach. It doesn't take him long to register what's happening as the police officers lift him off the ground and put handcuffs on his wrists.

Felix looks right at me with a smug smirk. "Tick-tock," he says as the police drag him away.

I don't have to ask what the meaning is behind his words. Kai's life is on the line. I have no idea how long I have to get to her. I don't know what danger and traps Felix may have set. Or if this is all a mind game he's playing with me.

All I know is I need to get to Alaska as soon as possible and pray that Kai is still alive by the time I get there.

10

KAI

"WE NEED to get you into bed," my father says.

"The doctor said I need to rest and take it easy for a couple of days, not that I need bedrest. All I've done is lay in a hospital bed for the last couple of days. Let's go sit out on the back porch and have some tea or something," I say.

My father frowns.

Beckett looks like I've just told him I want to go to a strip club and drink shots.

I sigh. "Fine, I'll rest for a little bit."

I shouldn't complain that I have two men that care so much about me. Even if they aren't the men I would prefer to have by my side. I'm beginning to trust them both. I'm beginning to think that either man would take a bullet for me or my baby.

I feel safe. If only Enzo...

No.

I won't let myself go there anymore. I don't get to look back, only forward.

All the people I loved are gone. These two men are my

future. My baby is my future. I can't think about anything else.

"I'll make you some tea though that you can drink in bed," my father says, kissing me on the forehead before heading to his kitchen.

Beckett holds out his arm to me.

I tilt my head to the side as I raise an eyebrow, but can't hide the light smile on my lips. "I can walk on my own, you know."

"What would Enzo do?"

I bite my lip as my full smile covers my lips. "He'd carry me to bed."

Beckett holds out his arms.

And my heart warms. Not in the flipping, beating kind of way it does for Enzo. More in the calm comfort way when Zeke or Langston would do something for me.

I take Beckett's hand, and he pulls me gently to him. A moment flashes, where I think I see a moment of reluctance from him. But as quickly as it comes, it's gone.

He wiggles his eyebrows, then scoops me up in his arms.

I giggle as he does. I haven't laughed much in the few weeks since I've been here, but he makes me laugh.

His phone buzzes as he carries me to the bedroom. And I see that slight frown again.

"Girlfriend problems?" I tease.

He slowly shakes his head as he carries me into my bedroom, "Kai, I need to tell you—"

"Put her down, now." The boom of the voice knocks us both back. I close my eyes as I feel the impact of those words. I don't trust my eyes. My eyes have imagined Enzo a thousand times. I don't trust my ears. My ears have sung his voice to me too many times. The only thing I trust is my heart. It can't be fooled. I focus in on my heart.

It beats, faster and faster. Skipping a beat in anticipation of being wrapped in his arms.

"Put the gun down. We don't need you getting trigger happy and shooting her. She's pregnant for goodness sakes," Beckett says.

Beckett is talking to the man. The man has a gun. *Is the man Enzo, though?*

My heart says, yes.

I open my eyes and see Enzo standing on the edge of the shadows of the room with a gun in his hand pointed at Beckett, who is still holding me in his arms.

"Enzo," I breathe.

He found me.

He came for me.

He should have stayed away.

Only one of us can live...

"Stingray," he says back.

"It's really you," I say, fighting to get out of Beckett's arms. But Beckett doesn't realize Enzo isn't a threat yet.

"Kai, when I put you down, I need you to get behind me. And make a run for the door if you get the chance," Beckett says calmly into my hair.

That's when I realize Enzo still has a gun pointed at us.

"Enzo, put the gun away," I say calmly, not sure why he's drawn his gun in the first place.

"No, Beckett is dangerous."

I look up at Beckett, who is holding me tightly.

"No, he's not. My father hired him as security. To protect me. Now, put the gun away."

Enzo doesn't drop the gun. "Put Kai down."

Beckett nods. "You're right. She shouldn't be involved in this."

Beckett walks us back to the door instead of toward Enzo.

"No!" I want to go to Enzo, not away.

Beckett turns his back to Enzo, shocking the hell out of me as he puts me on the ground at the door. "Run," he says.

I do run, just not in the direction he wants me to run.

I run right into Enzo's arms.

The gun lowers as Enzo wraps his arms around me.

We both exhale all of our pain at the same time as we hold each other. Everything we've been dealing with for the last few weeks is gone the second I hit his arms.

The fear.

The pain.

The ache.

All gone.

"I thought...I thought you were dead," Enzo says, tears flowing freely down his cheeks.

His hand brushes against my cheek as he runs his hand through my hair messily brushing it away from my face so he can look into my eyes—that are tear-stained and red.

We both forget about Beckett. All we see is each other.

Enzo grabs my neck and pulls me into the deepest kiss. A kiss that brings me back from the dead. A kiss that reminds me what love is and what I almost lost. A kiss that is more than a kiss, it's hope.

When Enzo pulls away, he's quickly brought back to reality. He grabs me and shoves me behind his body as he once again aims his gun at Beckett.

"Don't! He's on our side! He was just trying to protect me. He didn't realize who you were," I say, grabbing onto Enzo's arm, trying to get him to lower the gun.

Enzo narrows his gaze in Beckett's direction. "It was a brilliant plan. You fooled a woman who can spot a fraud from a mile away. But I know the truth. Tell her, so I can kill you."

Kill him? "No, you can't kill him," I cry.

Enzo looks at me like I'm breaking his heart for defending a man like Beckett. But I have no idea why Enzo is so insistent about Beckett. I'm rarely wrong about the character of a man. I can tell when I'm being lied to. I suspected Felix before anyone else did. And Beckett is a good man. He's saved me. Protected me. Even now, he won't draw his gun that I know he has because he's afraid of hitting me instead of Enzo.

"Beckett? Why does Enzo want to kill you?" I ask, when I see the reluctance in his eyes.

"Because he works for Felix," Enzo answers for him.

My jaw falls. "He doesn't. He can't..." but when I look into Beckett's eyes, I know it's true. He does.

"I'm so sorry, Kai. I wanted to tell you. I was going to and then—"

"And then nothing. We don't need to hear any more of your lies. Toss me your phone," Enzo says.

Beckett slowly reaches into his pocket and tosses Enzo his phone. Enzo pockets it.

"What was Felix's plan? How many others are here? How many people know Kai is here?"

Beckett stands tall and unafraid as he answers. Like he's willing to face whatever punishment awaits him. "Felix and I are the only ones who know. There is no one else here. He didn't trust anyone else with the information. He knew you could torture them into telling you where Kai was."

"What did Felix want you to do?" Enzo asks.

Beckett looks at me and sucks in a deep breath. "He wanted me to keep her safe until he gave the order to kill her."

So much pain in those words. So much hurt. I thought he was my friend—my protector. Instead, he was the enemy.

Enzo looks to me. "He's not your friend. He has to die for what he's done. What he was willing to do."

"Wait," I say. I need closure before he kills him. I need to look Beckett in the eyes and understand why. I walk out from behind Enzo, who grabs my arm as I go by. Not able to stand me leaving his safety for even a moment.

I squeeze his hand tightly and give him a knowing nod. And finally, Enzo lets me go. I walk over to Beckett and look into his eyes. But I can't trust my eyes. So I close them. I block everything out except my heart.

And I can still feel it. The calmness. The protectiveness. The conflict. There is more to Beckett's story than he's saying.

I open my eyes—they confirm what my heart feels.

I'm sorry, Beckett mouths to me. Not out of fear for his life, but because he's genuinely sorry.

Me too, I mouth back. And then I slap him hard across the cheek. "Don't ever lie to me again."

He nods, standing taller somehow. He's a tall man, easily an inch or two taller than Enzo. And then I see it— the missing piece to this story. Enzo doesn't see it yet. I'm not even sure if Beckett knows it. But neither is ready to talk about it now.

"Can I kill him now?" Enzo says.

"No," I answer.

"We can't trust him, Kai. I'm sorry if you've grown feelings for him, but the first chance he gets he'll go to Felix. And then you'll be a target again. I can't go through losing you again," Enzo says with so much heartbreak in his voice. And in this moment I regret not coming back. Not finding him in the weeks he thought I was dead. But I had to protect them both.

"Killing him isn't the only option," I say, walking back to Enzo so that he can relax a little. "Dad!" I shout, knowing that he is right outside the door listening.

My dad enters slowly, with his own gun drawn, aimed at Beckett.

Enzo smirks, like this proves he's right and that we should kill Beckett.

"I agree with Enzo, honey. Beckett betrayed us. He can't live," my father says.

"Well, I won't let either of you kill him yet. Every person in this room has betrayed me at one point or another. And I didn't kill either of you for it," I say.

Both Enzo and my father look wracked with guilt at my words. I hate throwing the past in their faces, but if it saves Beckett right now, I'll do it.

"Now, father go get some rope, something to tie Beckett up with," I say.

He frowns but nods, leaving to only return a few minutes later with rope.

"Enzo, grab his gun and any other weapons on him," I say.

"Hands up," Enzo says to Beckett.

Beckett puts his hands up as Enzo roughly searches him for weapons. When he's found two guns and three knives, he seems satisfied that he's found everything and takes the rope from my father and roughly ties Beckett's hands behind his back. Followed by his legs.

"Now what? What's your plan?" Enzo asks me with a tiny bit of snark to his voice.

"On the bed," I say to Beckett.

Beckett hops over to my bed and lies down.

"Tie him to the bed," I say to Enzo.

He takes the rope and ties Beckett to the bed in a sitting position with his arms behind his back. It's not the most comfortable position, but I don't want to deal with Beckett right now. I want Enzo.

I turn to my father. "Are you okay to watch him?"

He nods, holding his gun.

I put my hand on my father's chest. "Don't shoot him. Not unless you have to. Promise me," I say.

"I promise I won't shoot the lying bastard without your permission or if my or your life is on the line," my father says.

"Thank you," I say.

"Where are you going to go?"

I look at Enzo longingly. *Any place with a bed.*

"Remember what the doctor said," my father says with a cautious warning.

I smile. "I'll be fine. I'll call you tomorrow."

He reaches into his pocket and pulls out a key. "It's a gift —a house. I don't know how secure it is because Beckett knows about it. But it should be good enough for tonight at least."

I kiss him on the cheek with tears forming in my eyes again at the thoughtful gift that Beckett already showed me my father built for me so I would have my own space when the baby arrived.

"Thank you. Beckett showed me the house. It's beautiful. I can't thank you enough for it. It will be perfect for tonight," I say, taking Enzo's hand. I lead him out of the room. Out of the lies and betrayal. And into one tiny moment of happiness.

11

ENZO

As SOON AS we step out of the bedroom, my hands are all over Kai. Her face, her arms, her belly. I still can't believe she's alive. That this is real.

"You're alive," I cry, pulling her tightly against my body again.

"You're here," she cries back into my shoulder.

There are so many questions. So many things I want to know. But right now, what I need most is her in my arms.

The hug quickly turns into desperate kisses. *God, how I've missed her lips.* Her tongue dips into my mouth, and I swear I almost come from just her kiss. I never thought I'd feel this again. Never thought I'd feel love. Hope for the future.

Nothing will ever change that again. I will do whatever it takes to protect her. To protect the baby.

The baby!

Before I wouldn't talk out loud about the baby for fear if I did, something would go desperately wrong.

And then I remember what her father said about doing what the doctor said.

I stop the kiss. "What did the doctor say? Is my son okay?" I place my hand over her stomach, which seems triple the size it was the last time I saw her. Has it only been a few weeks?

She smiles. "I just had a little scare. Everything is fine, though. The doctor just said to take it easy for a day or two and not do anything that raises my blood pressure so high again."

The baby is fine. But that's a no for sex. I won't risk the health of the baby for my own selfish reasons. No matter how badly I want Kai right now.

Kai must be able to read my mind, though. "We have a lot to talk about, but not here. Is your car nearby?"

I nod. And then scoop her up in my arms. She smiles brightly like I just took the weight of the world off her shoulders as I carry her out of the small cottage.

"How did you find me?" she asks.

"Felix, he showed me a picture of you. I realized immediately that you went to Alaska. To the last place you thought anyone would think you would go to your father," I say.

She nods. "I thought the best place to go would be the last place Felix would look. I guess I was wrong."

I kiss her lips, to stop her from worrying about Felix.

"Felix is in jail. At least for now. I paid off enough people to put him in a max security prison. He'll be there for a while. Eventually, he'll find a way out, but I'll be notified when that happens. I think Beckett was telling the truth when he said he was the only one who knew where you were. As long as Felix can't contact him, then you're safe," I say.

She touches my cheek and then kisses me gently again.

Damn tears dance in my eyes again. "I missed you so much, stingray."

"I know. And I'm sorry for letting you think I was dead. I just—"

"Shh," I kiss her soft lips again. "I know. You did the right thing. It wasn't safe." It's still not safe. But for today, we are safe.

I carry her to my car hidden in the woods near the house. I still don't like that we are leaving Beckett behind even though he's tied up. And I don't trust her father any more than I trust Beckett. But Kai does. Something has changed between the two of them. So for now, I'll accept her judgment.

I set her down in the passenger side of the truck I rented. Seeming appropriate to handle the rough Alaskan terrain. And then I jump in next to her.

"Where are we going?" I ask.

She grins. "My house."

"Your house? You have a house?" I ask. I assumed she was living with her father. I didn't realize how settled her life had become here.

She nods. "My father saved all of his money for me. He bought this house; the rest is in a savings account for me. It was always meant to keep me safe. Beckett...I just saw it the other day."

She gives me directions, and I drive the couple miles through the woods to her house.

When I pull into the driveway, I wasn't expecting what I see.

"Your father bought you a mansion," I say.

She bites her lip and tucks her hair bashfully. "I guess he wanted to make up for all the crap he's put me through."

I stare at her. "This doesn't even begin to make up for what he did to you."

She nods. "It doesn't. But I genuinely think he is trying his best. I'll explain later. There is a lot to talk about. But right now, I want to forget about all the dangers and problems we will eventually have to solve. I want to forget about Felix and my father and Beckett and the Black empire. I just want tonight to be about us."

I lean over and kiss her lips gently again, trying not to get us both worked up when we can't do anything about it.

"But first..." she starts.

I suck in a breath waiting for what she's going to say.

"Langston and Liesel. Are they...?" She can't even finish the question.

I should say they are dead. It would protect them both more until they are safe that I'm the only person that knows that they are alive. But I can't put her through what I went through these last few weeks thinking she was dead.

"They are both alive."

She exhales the breath she was holding. "Really? They are both alive?"

I nod. "Yes, I've seen them both. Langston wasn't in great shape, though. I sent him away to recover. And Liesel wasn't safe. So they are both hiding. Both pretending to be dead."

"I know how that feels."

Why?

Was it because of Felix? Or something more?

But I don't ask, because right now it doesn't matter. What matters is being with her.

I get out of the car and walk over to the door. I open it for her and scoop her out as I carry her to the front door. I take the key from her and carry her over the threshold.

And just like that the mood changes. The spark between

us returns in full force. And I drive my mouth hungrily over hers at the same time her hands grip my hair, pulling me down roughly.

Kai nips at my lip as my tongue sweeps into her mouth. The kiss is everything and not enough at the same time. We both want more. Both desperate to feel alive again after both being dead for so long.

I can feel her heart thumping heavily in her chest, my own heart matching hers.

I have to stop this, my mind reminds me.

But my body can't.

"Kai," I say, sternly against her lips. "We have to stop. I have no control right now when I'm around you. And I won't hurt you. I can't."

Kai places her hand on my lips, and I slowly lower her to her feet, knowing we need some separation.

"Is there anything I can say that will end in you fucking me?" she asks.

I shake my head. "Your father was concerned. I know you're minimizing whatever happened at the doctor."

"So if I called the doctor who saw me, and they approved me for sex, then?"

My cock hardens painfully in my jeans, so desperate to be inside her.

"Yes, then I'd make love to you," I say.

She smiles at my change of words from fucking to making love. For us, it will always be making love. And as much as I want to fuck her hard on every surface in this house, I won't. I won't hurt her or the baby. But I do want to fuck her—slowly, gently taking my time, so the moment lasts forever.

She pulls out her cell phone and dials a number. "Hello,

doctor Aspen. I'm sorry to bother you; I just have one question I need answered."

The man must say something back, and then Kai asks, "Is it safe for me to have sex?"

She presses a button for speakerphone and then holds the phone out so we can both hear the answer.

"Yes, I don't see any problem with you enjoying intimacy. Just monitor how you are feeling and take it slow. But I would think it could actually help your anxiety and blood pressure."

She smiles brightly. "Thank you, doctor."

She ends the call.

She takes a step back, swaying her hips back and forth in the sundress she's wearing with a light sweater. She looks so happy and carefree.

"Are you coming to help me find a bedroom in this place or not?" she asks, stopping on the bottom step.

"Definitely coming," I run over to her, but she starts darting up the stairs, forcing me to chase her.

"That can't be good for the baby," I yell after her.

"Will you stop worrying? The happier I am, the better for the baby. And right now, I've never been happier."

I grab her from behind as she hits the top step. I wrap my arms around her hips and pull her to me. I sweep her hair off her shoulder and kiss her tenderly on her neck.

She gasps at the simple touch.

"Still want to play games with me?" I ask as I thumb her neck teasing her.

"No, I just want you."

I spin her around, and our lips collide again slowly, taking our time exploring each other's mouths as I walk her backward carefully toward the door at the end of the hallway. I'm tempted each time we pass a door to throw open the door and pray it's a bedroom. But I know the master is most likely at the end of the hallway, and I want the best room to be where I make love to her again for the first time.

Finally, we make it to the end of the hallway; I push open the door and break the kiss long enough to pull Kai into the room with me. When I flick on the lights, we both gasp at the sight.

The room is wall to wall windows that look like they fold back so the room can be completely outdoors. It backs up to the woods and a lake. And the lack of houses we passed on the way here tell me this room is completely private. There is a large deck off the back with a jacuzzi tub and another door that I assume leads to a bathroom.

Kai lets go of my hand long enough to walk over to the center of the bright white bed. She takes a seat on the edge as she takes in the scenery.

I want this to be perfect for her. So while she takes it all in, I fold all of the windows open, so it's like the forest becomes part of the room. Then I find a few matches in one of the top drawers. I pull them out and light the candles lining the floor all the way around the room. I light every one of them until the room is glowing with soft light and the forest beyond.

"It's so beautiful," she says. "I can't believe my father put this much thought into this house."

I nod. *I can't believe the bastard did either.* But I decide to keep my thoughts to myself.

I take her hand again, and she stands up. I consider my next move carefully. I want her. I love her. She's mine in almost every way except one. The one way that I've wanted for so long but have been too scared to make happen. I've been afraid of what it would mean for the Black empire.

Afraid of Felix coming along and destroying it. Afraid of what Kai would say.

But I'm not afraid anymore.

I'm more in love with Kai than I've ever been. And I can't wait another moment for her to not be mine forever.

So I pull the scrunchie off my wrist as I get down on one knee in front of her. Knowing that I need this, that we both need this, to feel whole. I want our first time together again to mean so much more than just reuniting—the start of a new life together.

"I love you, stingray, more than you will ever know. These past few weeks without you in my life have been the worst kind of torture. I'm not whole without you. I'm not me without you. I need you more than I need air to breathe. And I can't spend one more second where you aren't mine."

I untie the ring from the scrunchie—that contains three pieces that represent the most important men in her life— Zeke with the scrunchie, Langston with the ring, and me with the wooden heart.

"Truth or lies, you mean the world to me?" I ask.

"Truth," she says through tears.

"Truth or lies, I will never leave you again?"

"Truth."

"Truth or lies, I will protect you and our baby with my life?"

"Truth."

"Truth or lies, my heart only beats for you?"

"Truth."

"Stingray, will you marry me?"

12

KAI

"Stingray, will you marry me?"

I must have imagined those words. Those words can't be real. For the past few weeks, my life has been hell. My life has been figuring out how to get myself out of bed in the morning. How to put food in my mouth. How to survive without the man I love.

But it only takes a moment for everything to change.

I've experienced that enough times to know things can go from good to bad in an instance. Enzo knows that too.

But I'm discovering things can go from bad to good just as quickly.

I close my eyes and open them again, but Enzo is still kneeling in front of me in one of the most beautiful rooms I've ever seen.

This can't be real.

I shake my head, trying to get the image to change back to the darkness I'm used to, but no darkness comes. The light of the candles still shines just as brightly.

This can't be real.

Enzo takes my hand, his warmth shooting through my cold.

"This is real," he says, reading my mind.

I swallow hard, trying to clear my throat so I can answer him. I've never been more thrilled and terrified at the same time.

"Whatever dangers we will face, we will face them together. I won't let anyone hurt my family. Not you and definitely not our baby," he says.

And I believe every word. This time will be different. This time we will be together forever. This time we will both wear the last name—Black.

I can barely see Enzo through the tears falling down my face. But I don't need to see Enzo to feel him. Our connection is stronger than anything I've ever felt before. I know in my gut this is the only way either of us can move forward. The only way either of us can live—together, not apart.

Apart, we might be able to outrun our enemies. And together, we will have to stand and fight. But I'd rather fight every day to have the love of my life by my side, then run and be without him.

"Stingray?" Enzo says, still waiting for me to answer him with words. As if he doesn't already know the answer in my heart.

"Yes—yes, I will marry you!"

Enzo grabs me, wrapping me in his strong arms. He spins me around before setting me back down on the ground.

"Yes?" he asks again, needing me to say it again to make it real.

"Yes," I say with a giant smile.

His lips crush mine in a kiss I never want to end. But

Enzo does end it. He pulls away and holds out the ring lying on top of the scrunchie and wooden heart.

He takes the ring and places it on my finger. It's the same ring I wore before when we were fake married. The same ring his mother wore. A ring that means so much to both of us.

"Langston found it," he says.

I smile.

"My heart belongs to the devil," I read the inscription again.

Enzo's eyes darken.

I kiss his lips gently, "You may have started out as the devil, but you quickly became my angel."

He kisses back, hungrily. "I've still got plenty of devil left in me."

He takes my left wrist and places the scrunchie on it. "This got me through a lot of dark nights."

I bite my lip as I suck back more tears. "Langston, Zeke, and you. All the men that mean the most to me in the world." I look up in his eyes. "But you are the only man I can't live without."

Enzo grabs my cheeks, pulling me into a desperate kiss as I grab his neck, pulling myself up to match his kiss. This kiss is different than all our previous kisses. This kiss won't end. This kiss is the start of an unimaginable desire of lust flowing between us both. This kiss is the epitome of love. This kiss is everlasting. This kiss blows every other kiss out of the fucking water.

Enzo walks me back until I'm lying on the bed which might as well be a cloud in the heavens for how high I'm floating.

"I can't believe how perfect this is. This moment. It's like the world finally arranged to give us a happy ending for once," I say, looking around at the picture-perfect room.

Enzo kisses down my neck, sending familiar chills through my body from where his lips press against my sensitive skin.

"Not ending, beginning," he says.

"Beginning," I agree, already gasping and moaning although Enzo has barely touched me.

Enzo sits back staring at me in my dress I only now realize is white. And I know this is going to be more than just making love. This is going to be the beginning of our union together. We may not say the vows or sign the papers until later, but today in this bed with our bodies, we will become one. We will be married to each other in every way that matters.

"You look like an angel. Are you sure you're really here?" Enzo asks, stroking my cheek.

"This is real," I say, repeating his words from earlier. I grab the hem of his T-shirt and lift until I see the chiseled abs I've missed for so long.

"I'll never get enough of these," I say, kissing each hard ab individually, working my way up his chest until I reach his lips.

"And I can never get enough of these," he says, dipping my shirt down and exposing my breasts. His mouth wastes no time teasing each of them.

"I've missed your mouth, your tongue, your..." I can't think anymore as I feel his tongue flick across my sensitive nipple.

"These have gotten so big."

I nod. "Don't stop."

He continues to tease me with his tongue while I hold

his head to my nipples, unable to speak except in short, broken words or moans.

"I've missed these moans," Enzo says.

I see the hint of devil in his eyes as he stares down at my body. "This dress is too heavenly for the sin we are about to commit."

He grabs the dress and slowly rips it apart, exposing my entire body to him.

He bites his lip when he takes in my naked body. "You aren't wearing any underwear."

I grin as I sway my hips beneath his hungry stare. "It's like the universe fated us to be together today."

"I don't care if it's fate, karma, God, coincidence, or the stars that brought us together. I'm not letting anything rip us apart again," Enzo says.

"I need you—now."

"I'm already yours." But Enzo obliges my pleas. He stands and removes his jeans underwear quickly, discarding them before kissing over my naked body. My lips, my neck, my breasts, my swollen stomach, and then down between my legs. Teasing me with his tongue as a finger pushes past my slickness.

"You are so ready for me, baby."

"I told you—I need you, now."

He smirks against my clit. "Come."

I do, against his tongue and fingers. But it is nowhere near enough to satiate me.

"More," I beg.

He nods, silently agreeing to give me everything I've ever wanted.

He rolls me to my side and then lies behind me. Kissing my neck as he reaches around to taunt my sensitive nipples.

"Enzo," I cry, out of breath and needing him more than ever.

"I'm right here, baby." I feel his length pressing against my ass as he pulls my body to him.

I close my eyes as I can no longer see him anyway, and everything intensifies. I can feel every touch, every kiss, every breath like it was the first time he's ever touched me. Each and every moment gets sealed into my body, a memory no one can ever take from me.

"I love you, Kai."

"I love you, too."

And then I feel his cock pressing at my entrance. I open my legs wider, welcoming him in.

And it's everything.

My body is his. My soul his. My heart his.

And as quickly as I give, I get. I feel his everything filling me, making me whole. Giving me more love than I can ever return.

His cock drives into me over and over. Our bodies move together as the sparks fire off all over my body.

"You're mine, forever," Enzo says.

"And you're mine, forever."

Another thrust brings us both closer to climax. Closer to sealing ourselves to each other. Closer to becoming one.

"My husband, til death do us part."

"Yes, and you're my wife for as long as my heart still beats."

Enzo grabs my neck, pulling my face toward his as he tenderly kisses my lips.

Husband.

Wife.

We will sign the papers soon. Have a formal wedding even. But this is the day I became Enzo's wife. This is the day that I will remember forever as the start of us in this fight together—forever. This is the start of our happily ever after. Because I refuse to accept anything less than forever. Anything less than perfect.

One more thrust and we are both coming. Both floating high above all the danger. Both loving each other always and forever.

Enzo holds me tighter as we both come down from our high. Neither of us ever wanting to part from the other again. But as we have both learned good can turn to bad in an instant.

"Uh...Enzo," I say as the smell of something burning catches my nose.

"Mmm, I don't ever want to stop hugging you like this. You smell so good, you feel so good, you—"

"Enzo, I think something's burning."

Our eyes meet, his go wide, and he jumps out of bed. One of the candles has lit one of the curtains on fire.

Enzo grabs the curtain and wads it into a ball before stomping on it with his feet to put out the fire. But all the candles seemed to be working against us now as they begin singeing the walls and dripping hot wax onto the floor. Enzo races around the room naked, blowing out every single candle.

I laugh at how ridiculous it is, but then again, this is us. A couple of candles catching the room on fire barely seems like an inconvenience compared to what we've been through.

"What are you laughing at?" Enzo asks as he grumpily walks back to bed in the dark.

"You—I think I'm going to love our crazy life together. Thank you for rescuing me from the candles."

"Fire—I rescued you from the fire, that sounds more

manly," he says as he lays face down next to me, his hand rubbing over my belly.

I roll my eyes, "Fine, thank you for saving me from the fire."

Enzo kisses my belly as I rub my left hand through his hair, the ring finally back on my finger where it belongs.

"Oh my god! What was that?" Enzo says as he watches my belly dance.

I laugh at his reaction and take his hand. "The babies are kicking."

The look of awe on his face when he feels the kicking, floors me.

"Wait...did you say babies? Plural?" he asks.

I bite my lip as a huge smile takes over my face. "I found out the last time I went to the doctor. It's why my blood pressure was high, and my belly is so big already. We are having twins."

13

ENZO

"Twins?" I ask again after sleeping the entire night with her wrapped in my arms. I'm still not sure I believe that we are actually having twins. I can barely fathom having one kid, let alone two.

Kai laughs at my reaction. "I reacted the same way."

"Twins," I say slowly, like if I say it enough, it will make it more real.

I kiss her belly twice on each side.

"Do you know the sex?" I ask.

She nods. "Do you want to know?"

"Yes!"

She laughs again. "One boy, one girl."

"Jesus," I fall back on my heels, still reeling from having two babies. Two perfect babies—one boy, one girl. I've never been so happy in my entire life.

"And they are healthy?"

She nods, unable to contain her smile. *So beautiful.*

I kiss them again. "Mine."

One of them kicks at the sound of my voice.

"Wow," I say, pressing my hand over her stomach again.

"It's pretty unreal, isn't it?"

I grab her neck and kiss her again, not believing my life right now. Only yesterday, I thought I would never have this—a family. I thought Kai was dead. Our baby dead.

But then everything changed, and I get a second chance. I won't waste it.

"We should raise them here, in this house, far away from everyone else. Although, we may have to kick your father out of the state and do a background check on every person in the town."

She laughs. "I'm not kicking him out of town. But I don't think we can stay here, at least not forever."

"Why not?"

She sits up. "We have a lot to talk about."

I nod. I don't want to talk. I want to stay in our little bubble—forever.

I hand her my T-shirt to wear, and I put my boxers back on.

"Do you think your father stocked the house with any food?" I ask.

"Only one way to find out."

I take her hand and lead her out of the bedroom and down the stairs to the kitchen.

"Holy shit! I thought I'd never want to leave my house on the beach in Miami. I was a beach guy through and through, but being here and seeing this view out the window, I may change my mind," I say wrapping Kai in my arms.

She nods. "It's beautiful here, isn't it? I never thought I'd become a mountain girl either. But I've been as happy as I could be here these last few weeks."

I kiss her hair again. "I could get used to this—domestic

living. Get a normal job. Maybe become a fisherman or something."

She raises an eyebrow and laughs.

"What? You don't think I could be a fisherman?"

"No, you could. It's just the same job my father got when he moved here."

"Oh," I say, no longer wanting to become a fisherman. "Well, I'm sure I can get a boat and do whale watching tours or something."

She laughs harder. "You? A tour guide? You would be the grumpiest tour guide ever."

"Fine, well good thing we don't need money, then."

"Yes, because we would probably starve with you as a tour guide," she chuckles again.

I roll my eyes with a small grin as I walk to the fridge. There is a carton of eggs, and I spot some spinach, mushrooms, and tomatoes.

"Feel like an omelet?" I ask.

She makes a disgusted face.

"It's that or..." I open the pantry. "Donuts."

"Donuts!" she shouts.

I frown. "Are you feeding my babies anything but sugar?"

She laughs. "Yes, I am. Fine, make me an omelet topped with one donut."

I shake my head. "Fine."

I get the supplies out to start making two omelets in the gourmet kitchen, while Kai starts making coffee. Each time we do anything we brush against each other, or stop and kiss each other, just needing to touch each other as much as possible.

I finish making the omelets and Kai finishes making a cup of coffee for me and grabs a bottle of water for herself. I top her plate off with a donut, and then we sit out in the rocking chairs on the back deck overlooking the incredible view as the sun begins to rise.

"This is incredible! I don't even like omelets, but this is really good. Maybe you could get a job as a chef," she says.

I grin. "Maybe."

We eat in silence. Just enjoying the peacefulness of the fresh air and calm morning. Both of us imagining what our life would be like if we were any other couple. If we didn't come with baggage, enemies, and monsters. If we both didn't have fucked up fathers that messed us up worse than they messed up themselves.

This would be our life.

I'd wake up early every morning to make Kai breakfast. And be rewarded by seeing her walk around in my T-shirt.

We would go to normal jobs.

We would have friends that we wouldn't have to worry about their safety just because they are our friends.

Our kids could play in the yard without worrying about if our enemies were going to kidnap them.

But this isn't our life. This is just pretend. Because we have enemies. We have monsters ready to attack. This can never be our life.

Kai sets her plate down on the end table. I do the same. I pick up my coffee, and she grips her water bottle tightly.

"Truth or lie," she starts.

I suck in a breath. Our little moment of heaven is ending. This lie is over.

I nod for her to continue. Because I know whatever truths we will tell are going to be hard to face. We may not need to play the game to tell them, but it's more of a comfort thing than anything else. It lessens the blow somehow.

Reminds us both that even though Kai has only now agreed to marry me, we have always been connected to each other.

"Truth or lie, my father is actually my uncle," Kai says.

Holy shit. We aren't starting on something easy. None of this is going to be easy. This is going to be fucking hard.

"Truth," I say, completely broken for her.

She doesn't look at me, seemingly lost in that realization. "My birth father died in the final game."

Pain, so much fucking pain. I want to take it all away. But I can't. We could live a thousand lifetimes filled with only happiness, and it still wouldn't make up for the amount of pain we have both endured.

"My father was the devil. I'm so sorry, Kai."

I take her hand; she squeezes back. "Your turn."

"Truth or lie, I fought Langston thinking it was Felix."

"Lie," she says, giggling even though she knows it's the truth.

I shake my head. "Truth."

"How the hell did you mistake Langston for Felix?"

I shrug. "I was pissed off. I thought everyone was my enemy. And Langston wasn't in the best place. He thought everyone was dead. He couldn't deal with the pain."

I nod for her to continue.

"Truth or lie, Beckett is your brother," she says cautiously, like the words alone are going to torture me.

"Lie," I say, but as I say the word, I realize it's not true. Beckett could be my brother. He doesn't look much like me, at least, not in the obvious way. Not like Felix and Milo did.

But my life is filled with men that end up being related to me. It's possible. And the more I think about it, the more I realize it to be true. Beckett is tall, an inch or so taller than me. His hair blonde, his skin fair, unlike my dark hair and tanned skin. But he has my mother's eyes. Turquoise blue—warm and loving.

He clearly isn't afraid of death. He faced me without once drawing his weapon. And despite knowing differently, he seemed to genuinely care if Kai lived or died.

Beckett.

Finally, I realize why the name rings a bell.

"Beckett isn't his first name. It's his last name," I say.

Kai frowns. "How do you know that?"

"It was my mother's maiden name."

"So it's true?"

"Yes, Beckett is my brother."

Kai squeezes my hand again. "I know every brother that has entered your life has been out to get you. They have wanted power, revenge, money. But Beckett may have different motivations. He may be different."

I nod, I hope she is right. But I don't trust that any child that came from my father could ever be good, myself included.

"Truth or lie, I want to marry you today," I say, wanting to change to something positive.

Her eyes light up. "Truth."

"Marry me, today. I don't want to wait any longer."

She licks her lips as she considers. "I'll go to the court-house with you. I'll sign the papers and go through the motions. But when this is all over, I want a real wedding. With my father there. Any of your family there. With Langston and Liesel. And our children there. One where we can celebrate with everyone we love."

I smile. "You really forgave your uncle?" I don't understand why she still calls him father if he's actually her uncle.

Her nose twitches. "I believe in second chances. And he is the only grandparent our children have left. I think he loves me. I think he wants what is best for me. Even if he has fucked up in the past. I wouldn't say I've forgotten what he's done to me. But I forgive him. I'm willing to give him a second chance."

Second chances—that has been our entire life. I'm not sure I'm ready to give her father a second chance, but I can understand why Kai wants to.

But when I look in Kai's eyes, I know she isn't thinking about her father. She's thinking about her next entry for our truth or lie game, which at this point might as well be called truths. Neither of us can lie to each other anymore. And every truth she has spoken has been worse than the previous one. This next one is going to kill me. I can feel the change in her.

I tug on her hand, needing her as close to me as possible. She climbs into my lap. I brush her hair off her face, and she rests her head against my chest listening to my heart thump, thump, thump.

I hold her close, hoping the truth won't destroy what I just got back. *How could it?* I love her. We basically said our vows to each other last night. Nothing can destroy what we have.

But the tears falling down Kai's face, coating my bare chest say differently.

"Truth or lie," her voice breaks.

"Shh, it's okay, whatever it is, just tell me," I say stroking her hair. "Whatever it is, we can face it, together."

She swallows hard, refusing to let her fear win.

"Truth or lie, the final game is a fight to the death. The final game—only one of us can survive."

I let her words sink in. *No, that can't be true.*

But I know it is.

Only one of us can survive if the final game happens.

Everything makes sense now. Why the men wouldn't let us fall in love. To win the game, we have to fight each other to the death. It's why they want us to both have heirs before the final game. And it's why Kai's uncle raised her instead of her father. Her father didn't die in an accident. My father didn't kill him because he's a monster. He killed him because it was either her father or him. Only one could survive.

Was there a time when my father wasn't evil? Did the final game change him? Did killing a man he must have learned to respect over months finally cause him to crack? Is that what caused the monster to unleash?

Or was he always evil?

I'll never know.

But I know one thing—I won't let the final game happen. I'll kill Felix. I'll kill every man in the Black organization. No one will be left to force the last game to happen.

Then we will be safe.

Then we can have our happily ever after.

Only one can survive. But Kai and I are one. We will survive; everyone else won't if they step between us and happiness.

"What are we going to do?" Kai asks.

"Fight."

14

KAI

We put everything on hold after our talk. Enzo assures me Felix is still in a max security prison, although he can't guarantee for how much longer. Which means it's much more important for us to get married now. We want to be one in all the ways that matter.

I want a real wedding later, when this is all over. But for now, I need the piece of paper. I need the title. I need every tie to Enzo if he were to end up in the hospital. I want no doubt in our children's mind if something were to happen to Enzo and me that we loved each other more than life itself. I want them to know how hard we fought for them to have the life they deserve.

We have a lot of hard decisions to make in the future. A lot of impossible choices. But right now, we get another tiny piece of our happily ever after.

Enzo rented a small boat, and we drove it to the town over. A much larger town that has shops where we can buy rings, clothes to get married in, and most importantly, a courthouse where we can get married.

There is supposed to be a waiting period from the time

we get the license to when we can actually get married, but Enzo dropped me off at a dress shop while he went to persuade them with money, and I'm sure something more violent if they resist. I have no worries I will be able to get married today.

I walk through the rack of white dresses in the small dress shop. I chose not to go into a wedding dress shop. For one, I knew it would be hard to find a dress that fits me with my large bump. And two, it just didn't feel right.

None of these white dresses feel right either.

And then I spot the rack of black dresses. They call to me. Reaching into my dark heart and pulling me forward. I walk to the rack and pull the first dress off that I see.

It's black, has a high waist, and then flows all the way to the floor. The skirt is sheer, almost see-through, and there is a high slit up the side. I know without trying it on that it's perfect.

I get the dress, and then head to the lingerie store next door to pick out something sexy to wear underneath. If I'm going to get married in a courthouse, in a rush, while pregnant with twins, I'm at least going to look sexy as hell while I do it.

After picking out the perfect set of lingerie, I spot a jewelry store. I step inside.

"Can I help you?" the man behind the jewelry cases asks.

"Yes, I'm picking out a wedding ring for my soon to be husband."

He grins and pulls out a case of rings. "These are our most popular rings for men."

I spot the perfect ring immediately. "That one." I point to the simple black ring.

He picks it up and hands it to me. It feels warm in my hand, just like Enzo.

"Do you do inscriptions?"

"We do."

"Can you have one done in an hour?"

He nods. "For the right price."

I smile and pull off my own ring too. I hand them both. "Name your price." But I already know I will give this man everything I have, because today I'm marrying the only man I've ever loved. And to me, there is no price too high to make this day perfect.

―――――――

"ARE YOU READY? We are going to be late," Enzo says, knocking on the bathroom door of the hotel we rented for the night.

"Isn't it every bride's right to be late to her own wedding?"

"Yes, but since I had to bribe the judge to let us get married today, I don't think it would be wise to be late."

I grin and put the last red rose into my hair.

And then I step out of the bathroom. The look on Enzo's face is everything I was hoping for.

His eyes go to my dark black hair curled into long ringlets and stuck with red roses. They gaze over my sparkling green eyes and down to my red lipstick coated lips.

He stops breathing when he takes in the dress. The dress fits perfectly around my bump, as I knew it would. The sheer fabric is just see-through enough to see the hint of my bra and panties beneath the layers but not so see-through that I feel naked. And the slit shows off my long legs.

"Jesus effing Christ."

I laugh at his reaction. "What do you think?"

"I think it's not possible for any woman to look as beautiful as you do now."

I haven't had many opportunities to dress up. But today, I'm glad I had the perfect opportunity.

"If I didn't want to marry you so badly, we wouldn't leave this hotel room."

I blush and walk over to him. He's in a suit that fits him like a glove. I don't know how he managed to pull that off. But he did. He combed his hair back, and trimmed his beard down but didn't go completely clean-shaven, leaving just enough scruff on his chiseled jawline.

"Good thing I want to marry you just as badly, or I'd have you against the wall."

"Is that right?" he grins.

"Yes."

"Then I guess it's a good thing we are getting married today," he says, stepping toward me.

"I guess it is." I take a step, swaying my hips in the dress.

Another step toward each other.

Then another.

Then we are so close, but not touching. If we touch each other, we won't be getting married today. We will spend the rest of the day in this hotel room. So we don't touch, but that doesn't stop the electricity sparking back and forth between us. It doesn't stop the lust lingering in our eyes. It doesn't stop us from eye-fucking each other, slowing undressing each other with just our imaginations.

"We should go," Enzo says, his eyes staring so intensely at me I swear I could come just from his gaze.

"We should," I agree.

Enzo forces his eyes away first, pulling his phone from his pocket to look at the time. "We really need to go. We are supposed to be at the courthouse in five minutes."

"Lead the way, hubby."

He grins and holds the door open. "After you, wifey."

Once we have left the premises of the hotel, Enzo takes my hand when it's safe enough that we won't turn around and run back to the hotel to fuck each other's brains out.

We stroll hand in hand the three blocks to the courthouse, definitely taking longer than the five minutes we had left for our appointment. But I'm not concerned. Nothing can damper today.

We walk into the courthouse and into the room where we will be getting married.

I gasp at the sight.

It's covered in red rose petals. The lights have been dimmed, and there are only a couple of candles lighting the end of the aisle.

I look at Enzo, confused. "You did this?"

He nods. "I know it's not the fancy wedding. We will do that later with family and friends. But this is the one I will remember. This is when you become my wife. And I didn't want our memories to be of a crappy courtroom. I wanted it to be as beautiful as you look."

"Thank you," I say, doing a good job of keeping my tears at bay even though I'm very emotional right now.

Enzo holds out his elbow to me. I take it and walk down the aisle with him as soft music plays.

We reach the end, and the judge starts talking about love and what a commitment marriage is. I realize two strangers are standing next to us.

"Our witnesses," Enzo whispers into my ear as he takes both of my hands.

I remember back to our first fake marriage.

How lucky am I that I get to marry Enzo not once, the fake marriage, not twice, now, but three times, our future ceremony?

"What?" Enzo asks with a grin. Neither of us is listening to the officiant, much like our first fake marriage.

"Just thinking about the last time I was marrying you."

"I was stupid not to marry you for real then."

"No, this is perfect."

The officiant turns to Enzo. "Do you Enzo Black, take Kai Miller to be your lawfully wedded wife, for sickness and health, for richer or poorer, til death do you part?"

Black, Enzo used Black as his last name—not Rinaldi.

I grin. Happy that he used the name I've always known him to be. I'm not sure if Enzo's legal last name is Black or not. But I have no doubt he has papers—passports, birth certificates, etc. that say his name is Black.

And I want to be Kai Black, not Kai Rinaldi.

"I do," Enzo says.

"And do you Kai Miller, take Enzo Black to be your lawfully wedded husband, for sickness or health, for richer or poorer, til death do you part?"

"I do."

"You may now exchange rings as tokens of your love and symbols of your marriage."

Enzo reaches into his pocket to pull out the box I brought back from the jewelry store. I didn't let him open it until now. I wanted the rings to be a surprise.

He thought I was crazy. But he kept to his word.

He opens the box, and I grab the ring I bought Enzo.

"With this ring, I'm yours forever. I'm your wife. Your

lover. Your savior. Your protector. Mother of your children. Your everything. Forever."

I slide the black ring I picked out and had inscribed onto his finger.

"My heart belongs to stingray," Enzo reads the inscription with tears in his eyes. "It's perfect."

Then he takes the other ring from the box, the one his mother wore all those years, and takes my left hand.

"With this ring, I vow to put you and our children first forever. I vow to be a loyal husband worthy of you. I vow to love you all of my days. I promise to protect you from all the evil that comes for us. I promise to never let another man hurt you. I vow to make up for all the mistakes of my past. I vow to be the father our fathers never were. With this ring, I'm your husband, forever."

He slides the ring onto my finger. And then I read the inscription that belonged to his mother along with the one I added.

"My heart belongs to the devil, aka Black."

Enzo's thumb brushes across the black ring as a tear drops down on top of it. I look up and see Enzo's tears dripping down his face onto our joined hand.

"Happy tears, I promise," he says.

I grin. "The happiest."

And just like that, everything else fades. It's just us. And the need to be joined in our own way outpaces everything else.

We forget we are standing in a courtroom Enzo decorated for our wedding. We forget two strangers are standing next to us watching us. We forget there is an officiant standing two feet from us.

It's just us. The two of us about to be the four of us. Enzo's lips crash down on mine, cementing our new relationship before the officiant has a chance to say we are man and wife.

The kiss brings up every emotion I've ever felt for this man. Love, passion, desperation, lust, anger, sadness, fear. They all creep up in my veins and explode out in this kiss.

Both of us kiss like we didn't just make a declaration of love in front of the world. Instead, this kiss needs to prove our love. And if this is how we prove our love, I want to spend our life proving it over and over again.

"I now pronounce you husband and wife," the officiant says hurriedly before scurrying off.

Enzo laughs against my lips. "I think we scared the officiant and witnesses off with your moaning."

"I was not moaning."

"Really? Then what do you all those cute little sounds you make when I kiss you?"

He kisses me again, then moves down my neck so my moans can be fully heard.

"Happiness, I call them happiness."

He smirks and devours my lips again. His hand slides through the slit of my dress, and up my thigh. He hooks his thumb in my black panties and starts pulling down.

A moment of clarity stops me. "Enzo, we can't! We are in a courthouse."

He bites my bottom lip, pulling it roughly into his mouth and I'm goo. I'm putty in his hands. I will fuck him here. I will fuck him in a filthy bathroom. I will fuck him in the park outside where everyone can see. I don't care.

He nuzzles his head against my neck. "You were saying?"

"Fuck me, Black."

"I thought you wanted to wait until we got back to the hotel room? I had the room decorated with rose petals, candles, the whole works."

I shake my head as surges for desire shoot through me. "I can't wait."

His eyes darken, as he slips a single finger in my panties and presses against my clit.

I about come at his single touch.

He chuckles, his voice deep and heavy. "You can't wait."

"Take me, Black."

I hear rustling at the door, and I know someone is about to enter—possibly a guard about to throw us out.

But I know it won't stop Enzo. We want each other too badly. Nothing will stop this from happening.

"Do you trust me?" he asks.

It's a question he's asked me before. But I've never trusted him more than I do now.

"Yes."

He gets a devious look in his eyes, and I know I'm in trouble.

Enzo lifts me up into his arms and kisses me again. "I will never get enough kisses from you, Mrs. Black."

I sigh. "I will never get used to you calling me that."

"You've earned the title, in more ways than one. You're my wife. My partner. You could run the Black organization as well or better than I could."

I run my hand across his jaw. "Definitely better," I tease before nibbling on his bottom lip.

"You are going to pay for that, wifey." He slaps my ass as he carries me through a door I didn't notice at the back of the room.

We close the door just as I hear a guard enter the room.

"Anyone in here?" the man shouts in the courtroom. I realize we are in what looks like a tiny office, most likely for the judge.

I start giggling as I hear the guard continue to shout in the room.

Enzo puts a finger over my lips, trying to silence me, but it's not enough.

"You're going to get us caught," Enzo whispers into my ear through my hair.

My eyes shine because I know that's not possible today. Today the universe is finally on our side. Today nothing can touch us.

"Oh really, you are scared of getting caught?" I tease.

I grab the belt around his waist and undo it. Then I take my time undoing the button and pulling down the zipper.

I still hear the guard's footsteps in the other room, but that only emboldens me more. Because I truly think the world is finally on our side. I think I could scream right now and the guard would mistake it for a bird. Nothing can touch me.

Enzo's eyes follow my every movement. His gaze alone warms my entire body. *How can one look do so much to my body?* I don't understand the human body, but I do know one steely glance from Enzo, and I'm panting, hot, and lusty. I want everything he is offering behind his dark brown eyes.

I reach into his pants and free his cock, which has already hardened. I hold it carefully in my hand as I kneel in front of it. My eyes look up as I flick my tongue over the tip of his veiny cock.

"Jesus, stingray," he says as his eyes roll back in his head.

I love how I affect him like this. I could stay here on the floor, sucking him off all day.

But quickly he's a grabbing my arms and pulling me up. "My queen doesn't kneel in front of me. You deserve to be worshipped."

I open my mouth to say I love kneeling in front of him if I get to suck his delicious cock.

But he doesn't let me speak. His lips kiss mine, taunting and teasing, but never letting me get the full taste of his tongue I want.

He walks me back until I feel the edge of the desk behind me.

"Stop teasing me," I whisper.

"You started it," he says.

I grab his cock in my fist again, stroking once slowly, trying to get back some of my power.

He purrs, putting his hands on either side of the desk boxing me in as he savors the pleasure I'm giving him.

I like this—feeling like a goddess. Feeling powerful.

"I like you in this tuxedo. You look dabber," I say, stroking his cock again as I adjust his bowtie.

He grabs my hand over the bowtie and rips it from his neck. We are done playing games with each other. This is about to get serious. He loosens the collar of his shirt as I rip off his jacket.

And then he grabs my hips and sets me on the edge of the judge's desk.

"We are so going to hell for this," I say.

He spreads my legs as he rips my panties off. "Good thing we were already going to hell anyway."

I gasp so loudly I'm sure the entire courthouse can hear me. "At least we aren't doing this in a church."

"Oh, I plan on fucking you in every building, alleyway, meadow, car I can find, and churches aren't excluded from that."

"You should have included that in the vows."

Enzo dips his tongue between my legs, and I no longer

have words. I lean back, resting on my hands as he takes his time devouring my pussy.

"I promise it to you now. Your pussy will never be safe from my tongue or cock. I will make you come every chance I get. I will never let anything come between me and making you orgasm. This I vow."

I want to laugh, but the serious look on his face tells me this vow is as important to him as all the rest of them.

He grins when he notices the heavy rise and fall of my chest. My nipples harden beneath the thin material of my bra.

"Scream my name, baby," Enzo says, pushing two fingers inside me as his tongue teases my clit again.

"Yes, Enzo!" I scream loudly enough to rattle the building.

I glance over at the door for a second. We didn't even bother locking it. But no one comes. I swear I hear footsteps outside the door, but none draw closer.

I grin. "We really are in our own little world."

But then, Enzo is licking quickly over my clit. All my blood has headed south, intensifying every touch of his mouth on me.

"I'm going to..." but I can't finish the sentence. I come hard on Enzo's tongue and fingers—spilling my wetness all over the desk.

Enzo stands, licking his fingers clean as his needy gaze stares down at me.

"More," I say. His cock is still erect and needy. And one orgasm isn't enough to satisfy me. I don't care that we have a perfectly good hotel room a few blocks away. I need Enzo now.

He holds out his hand. I take it, and he helps me off the desk. Enzo eyes my swollen belly that I automatically hold with my hand when I stand up. With each day that passes, I know sex is going to get harder and harder. But I have faith nothing will stop Enzo from giving me a daily orgasm. He just promised as much five minutes ago.

"You are the sexiest woman I've ever seen. And seeing you grow my babies inside of you does things to me you will never understand."

I love how he never doubts the babies being his. He never brings up the fact that they could be Milo's. They are his. In every way that matters. And the fact that every time Enzo speaks the babies move and kick in my stomach brings me more peace than anything else. Because they know he is their father too.

He takes my hand and spins me around like I'm a princess he's twirling. My dress flies up as I spin. He grabs the material, pushing it up high on my hips as he backs me up to his cock.

I grab the desk for support as I push my ass into his cock. He drives inside of my slickness quickly. Both of us so desperate to feel each other that we can't take another moment apart.

"I can never get enough of this. This first moment when you slide inside me is everything," I say.

He kisses my neck as his hands move around to my front, supporting my heavy stomach in his hands. "I can never get enough of you, wife."

Tingles flicker down my neck as he says, wife.

"Fuck me, husband."

He growls. Loving me calling him husband as much as I love him calling me wife.

And then he fucks me hard and fast. His teeth sink into my neck, teasing me with just the right amount of pain as his teeth touch my sensitive skin.

"Mine," he says, fucking me harder.

"Yours," I cry back.

I can never get enough of his cock. Of his hard body slamming into me. I love every way he fucks me. Hard and fast. Slow and tenderly. It makes no difference to me. I love it all. I love him. I can never get enough.

"More," I beg.

Enzo pushes his cock deeper inside me. And my body becomes his. His to own, to love, to cherish.

"I love you, wife."

"I love you, husband."

I come hard on his dick. And he spills his cum deep inside me.

Carefully, he pulls out. "Did I hurt you? I lost a little control back there." Enzo rubs the spot on my neck where his teeth sunk into my neck. And then he quickly examines my body for some sign that he hurt me.

I laugh still floating high in my orgasm cloud. "You could never hurt me. Only with your last breath could you ever cause me pain."

"The babies?" he asks, in a panicky voice.

I grab his hand and press it over my stomach where they seem to be dancing in my belly. "Are happy."

He exhales his breath and then kisses me. "I never want to hurt you again."

"So you never will. The only way you can hurt me is by leaving me."

He nods.

We hear more footsteps outside and light voices.

"We should leave," Enzo says.

I smile as I look around the small room. It felt like the perfect place to celebrate being husband and wife.

I pull my dress down and slip my panties back on, while

Enzo does his pants up and buttons up his shirt. He doesn't bother with the tie; he just shoves it in his pocket. And then he drapes his jacket over my shoulders when I shiver.

We walk to the door, and Enzo cracks it open. Another couple is walking in, in awe of the decorations Enzo did.

I'm happy another couple gets to enjoy them.

"Come on, let's go before we get trapped watching another boring wedding ceremony," he says.

"Boring? Did you think our ceremony was boring?"

He laughs. "No, but another ceremony happened when I was fucking you. Didn't you hear them? You came as they said I do."

I giggle. "No, all I heard was you."

He kisses me. "And that's exactly what I wanted."

He takes my hand, and we walk out. The officiant doesn't look surprised to see us, but the couple walking down the aisle seem confused.

"If you get a chance after, I highly recommend trying out the desk in the back," Enzo says, winking at the couple.

I laugh and tug him out of the courthouse before we get in trouble.

Once out in the warm sun, Enzo asks, "Back to the hotel? A stroll through town first? Food?"

"Hotel," I say, not nearly satiated after one round.

He grins. "Did I tell you I love you?"

"Not enough."

"I love you, stingray."

"I love you too, Black."

Enzo grabs my left hand with his left hand and brings both of our ringed fingers to his lips and kisses my ring.

"Let's go," he says.

We start strolling casually back to the hotel, when everything changes.

133

Enzo's phone buzzes. He shows me the name that pops up—my father's name.

"Hello," I say when Enzo puts the phone on speaker so I can hear.

"Beckett escaped," my father says.

And just like that our fairy tale ends.

15

ENZO

Kai thinks the world is on our side. That fate has finally turned. That we are destined to be together. That nothing can rip us apart.

I love her positive thinking. It keeps me grounded, the anxiety and fear at bay when I'm with her.

But I disagree with her. I don't think anyone is on our side. I still think the world is against us. I see every person as an enemy, a threat about to attack us.

Kai thinks we are untouchable on our wedding day— the world wants to celebrate with us.

But with one phone call, that joy and hope are wiped out.

"Beckett escaped," Kai's father says.

I grab the phone and shove it to my ear, even though it's on speaker. I want to go through the phone and punch Kai's father for letting this happen. He had one job. Keep Beckett prisoner through the weekend. We would come back on Monday and decide what to do with him.

"You had one job," I growl through the phone.

"I know. I don't understand how it happened. I never let

him out of my sight. He was always tied up, and I barely gave him enough water and food to survive."

"Then how did it happen?"

There is a silent pause. "I let my anger get the best of me. I punched him. He was able to overpower me so close."

"Fuck."

"But he didn't escape then. I got him tied back up, and then I went to get some ice for my eye. I have no idea how he did it. It would take a Houdini to get out of those ropes. But he escaped."

"Fuck!" I growl louder. Passerbyers stop and give me a dirty look for my swearing. I snarl back at them as Kai frowns at the phone. Clearly as pissed off as I am about her father letting Beckett escape.

"Did he have help?" I ask.

"I honestly don't know."

"Do you have security footage?"

"Yes, but not of that room. Just of the perimeter."

"Send it to me."

"Done. What do you want me to do now?"

I want to search for Beckett myself. I'm the only one I trust, but I don't want to leave Kai unguarded. So I won't. I won't leave her.

"Find him." I hang up the phone.

Kai frowns. "This doesn't mean the world has turned against us. And it doesn't mean my father doesn't care about me. He didn't let Beckett go on purpose."

I pull up the security footage he sent me. I watch Beckett sneak out of the house, grab Kai's father's car, and take off.

"No, I don't think your father let Beckett go on purpose. He's just incompetent."

She nods. "So what now?"

"First, we get off the street." I take her hand. There are only two hotels in this town. I want to go back to our room, but it would be too easy for Beckett to find us there if he is searching for us. So I start walking in the direction of the other hotel.

"Where are we going?"

"To a different hotel. Beckett will still be able to find us if he wants to, but it will slow him down. He'll stop at the hotel where I used my credit card and real name first. This will give us a bit of a head start if he is searching for us."

"He's not coming for us. I truly don't think he would hurt me," she says.

I pull her into my body. "If he does come, I won't let him hurt you."

Her eyes flicker up. "And I won't let him hurt you either," she growls back equally as determined as I am to protect her.

"You aren't going to make protecting you and the babies easy are you?"

"I won't put myself at risk because of the babies, but I won't just stand by and watch you die if it comes to it. These babies need their father."

I link hands with her again, feeling the cool metal from her ring on mine. At least we are married now. There is nothing that will break us apart again. I'm sure of it.

We walk quickly down the street, but we stick out like a sore thumb. If Beckett is already here, he will notice us in a second.

The two towns aren't close together, though. It took us over an hour to get here by boat. We have time to get off the street and make a plan that involves sneaking through the shadows out of here.

We stroll into the lobby of the second hotel hand in hand. Both of our eyes scanning for danger at every turn.

Kai tries to turn us toward the front desk, but I stop her and head straight for the elevator.

"What are we doing? We don't have a room here," she says.

"I know, but I don't have enough cash on me to pay for a hotel room. And I don't want any trail for Beckett to follow. We just need a room to duck into for a moment. We aren't staying."

Kai nods as the elevator doors open on the fourth floor. I duck my head out and find exactly what I'm looking for. A maid outside one of the hotel rooms with her cart.

"Do you want me to or—" I start.

"I got this," Kai says.

I smile and grip her hand, so she is on the side closest to the maid. I love how I don't even have to communicate what my plan is; she's already on the same page as me. And I love how our skills compliment each other.

"Have I told you how much I love you?"

She looks at me and giggles, gushing at me, pretending I'm the only person she sees.

I watch from the corner of my eyes as the maid stops folding the towel she is holding and sighs at us.

"We just got married today," I say to the maid as we approach. "I'm the luckiest guy in the world."

"You two look very in love," the maid says, smiling brightly.

I don't know if Kai snatched the maid's key card or not. But Kai doesn't stop me as I nod at the maid and keep walking, so I assume she did.

We walk ten more doors down before Kai holds the key card out. We stop in front of a door as the maid heads back inside the room she is cleaning. We both listen at the door. I knock lightly. No one answers. So we insert the key and go into the small room.

It's unoccupied. We spot no signs of anyone staying here.

Kai wraps her arms around my neck and kisses me hard and passionately, like she's afraid this will be the last time she will ever kiss me. As much as I enjoy the kiss of her slick tongue, my erection pressing between her legs. This can't happen now. Not until I get her somewhere safe.

"Hold on, baby." I kiss her gently, trying to get her to calm down.

"I want you so badly."

"I know, I want you too. But I have to get you somewhere safe first."

She nods, taking a deep breath to try and calm down. "Beckett won't hurt me. Or you."

My lips thin. I wish I saw the good in people the same way she does. But I don't. Every person is as equally capable of good and bad. Everyone is shades of gray. Every once in a while you might find a truly bad apple. One who is only evil. But I've never seen a person that is pure good.

"Beckett is my blood. No one that comes from the Black line is all good. We all have a little evil in us," I say.

"Our kids won't," she says, rubbing her stomach.

"Only because they will take after you and not me."

She rolls her eyes. "You have plenty of good in you."

"And also plenty devil."

"So what's the plan? My father is searching for Beckett. But since he let Beckett escape, I'm not sure he's capable of finding him. What is our big concern here? That he will contact Felix or some of Felix's men to come after us?"

I nod. "You're right. Felix is still our biggest concern—

not Beckett. But since Beckett works for Felix, we can't let any of them know where we are." I wish Langston was here. He'd find Beckett in minutes.

"Should we search for Beckett?" Kai asks.

Yes.

But I look at her stomach, and I won't put her in danger. I don't know when her due date is, but it's only a couple of months away. I won't risk stressing her or the babies out. I could find Beckett easily, but I won't bring Kai with me. And I won't be away from her.

"No, we will give your father a chance to find him. But we can't stay here. Beckett has probably already contacted Felix. I'm sure Felix has sent men here to hunt us down. Felix only let you live because Beckett was monitoring you."

"So where do we run?"

I frown. I don't like running. We need to face Felix. We need to face the rest of the Black organization. Or at least, I do. But I won't let her get hurt in the process. What's most important right now is keeping her safe until the babies are born. Once they are here, I will gather an army to help me take out Felix and the rest of his crew.

"The water," I say.

She smiles. "The ocean."

There is a knock on the door.

Kai's eyes widen. And my heart stutters.

It's probably just the maid, but it's enough to cause both of us panic.

I motion for Kai to go in the bathroom as I draw my gun. She creeps carefully inside as I walk to the door. I hold the gun out as I look through the peephole.

Beckett.

He holds his hands up. "I'm not armed. I'm here to protect Kai, as I promised."

I look to Kai in the bathroom. "Lock the door," I tell her.

She closes the door, and I wait until it's locked. Not that that will stop Beckett if he wants to get to her. I'm the only thing stopping him from getting to her.

And this time, I won't pause if Beckett threatens Kai. I'll kill him. I don't care that he's my brother.

I flick open the door with my gun aimed at his head. Beckett kicks his gun to me on the floor, his hands still in the air.

"Get inside," I say, even though I want him as far away from Kai as possible. I don't trust him. Even if Kai sees something good in him. He might not be as bad as Felix. But I saw the way he looked at Kai. He has feelings for her —lustful feelings. All men are dogs. Beckett is no different. I won't let him touch her.

Beckett walks carefully inside. I close and lock the door behind me as I keep the gun on him as he walks and sits down the bed.

He stares at my attire. "Did I miss the wedding?"

"What are you doing here?"

"I came to warn you."

"Warn me that you escaped? Yea, I got the message. Now tell me something that will keep me from putting a bullet in your head."

I hear the unlock of the bathroom door.

"Kai, I told you to stay in the bathroom," I say.

She walks over to me. "And since when do I ever take orders from you?"

I sigh.

"What are you doing here, Beckett?" she asks, her arms crossed. She's pissed. "You ruined my wedding day, after all. I should be honeymooning right now, not deciding whether you should live or die."

I smile, at least she's on my side now about whether Beckett should live or die.

"Felix is out," Beckett says.

I frown and pull my phone out. But my contact in the prison hasn't contacted me. "How do you know?"

Beckett puts his hands down on his lap. "Because he contacted me."

"I took your phone."

"No, you took one of my phones."

I frown. *Such a rookie mistake.* I should have searched him better.

"I escaped your father, who you need to teach how to keep a man captive better. I could have escaped long ago if I wanted to."

I give Beckett a stern look, and he gets back on track.

"Felix contacted me. Told me he is coming to Alaska. That it's time to move in before Kai gives birth."

"Shit."

Kai's mouth drops. "Felix is on his way here."

"And he's bringing an army. He's ready to fight."

"Fuck," I run my hand through my hair trying to formulate a plan. I need to contact any men I trust. I need to gather my own army. I need a fortress to protect Kai. This can't be happening.

"I already have a plane that will take you to a yacht two hours from here. From there, you can disappear."

"Whose yacht?"

"One of yours."

We need to move. I know that. But our next move is the difference between us living or dying. Whatever decision we make is critical. Do we trust Beckett's intel? Do we trust that Beckett has arranged a flight and a yacht for us and hasn't told Felix about our escape plans? Or do we try to come up with some plan on our own—with limited resources and time?

I look at Kai who is staring at Beckett closely, trying to determine the same thing.

"Why are you telling us this?" she asks, her voice calm, yet stern.

Beckett's eyes lighten as he looks from Kai to me. "Both sides reached out to me almost simultaneously. I was working as a private investigator and bodyguard before all of this. But your father and Felix both reached out to me to work for them within days of each other. The money from each was too good to pass up, and I could do both jobs for a while. Eventually, I knew I would have to choose, to betray one side for the other. I figured I would just be loyal to whoever offered more money, more adventure. I needed excitement and a break from my pathetic life before this."

Beckett's eyes cut from me back to Kai. "But then, I met you. And everything changed. I don't know why I chose your side, or even when, but I did. It's just this feeling deep in my gut that says I need to do this. That I've always belonged on this side. This is where I'm supposed to be."

Kai touches his arm and gives him a tight smile. She has feelings for him. Not like she does for me. But like she did for Langston and Zeke. She sees him like a brother. She trusts him. But I'm not sure I believe Beckett's bullshit story.

I cross my arms staring down at him with threatening eyes, letting him know if anything happens to Kai or the babies, he will be the one to pay. Whether it's his fault or not.

Beckett looks up at me with determined eyes. "There is a reason both sides approached me within two days of each other. Some connection I'm missing. But I know it wasn't a coincidence."

Because you are my brother, but now is not the time to say it out loud. All of my brothers have betrayed me in the past. Beckett will be no different.

Right now, I don't think we have a choice. Felix is on his way here with an army. Beckett is offering a plane and a yacht. The only way we get screwed over is if Felix is already on the yacht when we get there. But if he's not, and Felix is just tracking us through Beckett, I'll end him before Felix can use Beckett to get to us. Felix may have the advantage on land, but on the sea, I will win.

Kai looks at me, and we exchange a silent conversation back and forth.

Are we going to trust Beckett? I ask, silently.

Kai takes a deep breath and then nods.

She's a great judge of people. She saw that Felix was evil before I did.

I don't trust Beckett as far as I can throw him. But Kai does. We are in this together. I don't get to make the decisions for both of us anymore.

"Trust me," she whispers.

I nod. I trust her.

I take her hand and give it a squeeze. It doesn't matter if Beckett is good or evil. I will protect Kai and our babies from any monster, even my own brother.

16

KAI

Enzo doesn't trust Beckett.

But he trusts me.

And I trust Beckett. I feel the same warmth off of him that I feel when I'm around Langston.

Beckett is on our side. Enzo finally has a family member in the family whose heart is the same as Enzo's. A person who could actually grow to love us, become part of the family. We just all have to live long enough for Enzo to tell Beckett the truth, and for Beckett to prove to Enzo that he's on our side.

"I want your gun," Enzo says to Beckett.

"Enzo," I say his name as a curse. "If Felix is after us, we need him to be able to fight back, same as us."

Enzo frowns. "And I need to focus on shooting Felix and his men, instead of worrying that Beckett is about to shoot us in the back."

Beckett pulls out his gun and hands it to Enzo. "Get off your high horse, man. Don't act like I'm the only one who has ever been on the wrong side. I've just never fucked up as badly as you did."

Enzo punches Beckett hard in the face for that comment.

I wince but don't try to stop the fight. They are grown men. And I think Enzo punching Beckett could actually be a good thing. Get out a little of his frustration.

"You risked my wife and children's lives. If you do it again, I will kill you," Enzo says.

Beckett smirks, and the similarity between his and Enzo's grins is astronomical. *How did I not see it before?*

"Now that you've gotten that out of your system, can we go to the airport?" Beckett says, trying to take control.

Enzo gets in Beckett's face. "You are not in charge here, asshole."

Beckett pushes back. "I am when I'm the one with the plan to get us out of here without Felix finding us."

"Guys, we don't have time for a pissing match. We need to get moving. No one is in charge. We all make decisions together," I say.

Enzo backs down, but the scowl never leaves his face. I cut him some slack because I know he has trust issues, and this is hard for him trusting a man like Beckett. He wasn't there when Beckett held my hand and pretended to be Enzo when I was in the hospital worried about losing the babies. He was there for me when Enzo couldn't be. You can't fake that kind of emotion. Beckett cried tears of relief right along with me when the doctor told me I was having twins.

But Enzo wasn't there. He doesn't share that history. It will take him time to open up, and I won't push him.

"I wish we had time to change," I say, still wearing my black wedding dress. Enzo is still in a tuxedo. The only person that looks inconspicuous is Beckett dressed in jeans and a flannel shirt. His sleeves are rolled up, and I can barely make out the tattoos covering his arms.

"Me too," Enzo says, taking my hand.

But we don't have time. And we don't have any clothes to change into. We will just have to make do until we can pick something up.

"Let's go," Enzo says.

Enzo leads the way out of the hotel. We try to walk calmly, instead of running like we want to.

Once on the street, Beckett motions to follow him. We do and find ourselves driving in a pickup truck to the small airport.

He hands us each a ticket. "Sorry I couldn't arrange a private flight. But this flight leaves in twenty minutes. If we hurry, we'll make it."

I stare at the tickets he handed Enzo and me. The seats aren't together.

Enzo growls when he realizes.

"I'm sure you can ask someone to swap with you, but these were the only seats left," Beckett says. He jumps out of the truck, and we follow.

Everyone stares at us in the small airport, our attire making us stick out way too much in the crowd of flannel, jeans, and boots.

Enzo tries to lean into our appearance, slinging his arm over my shoulder and kissing me often so that it appears we are headed to our wedding or honeymoon. Instead of running for our lives. We don't need anyone gossiping about us and making it easier for Felix to find us.

We board the plane, and before we even get to the seats, Beckett has already convinced people to move seats so Enzo and I can sit together.

"Thank you," I mouth to Beckett, who is sitting a few rows back before I take my seat.

Beckett gives me a curt nod in return.

"See? Becket is trying," I say to Enzo.

Enzo just grunts and takes his seat next to me in the small plane.

I sigh and grip Enzo's hand as the plane takes off. Step one went off without a hitch. No Felix or his men in sight. I just hope the next step goes just as smoothly.

I place my other hand over my stomach as the babies start kicking again. *Please, let me be doing the right thing.*

I glance over my shoulder and see Beckett watching Enzo and me closely. *To protect us or destroy us?*

I close my eyes, and everything in my body screams—protect us. Beckett is here to protect us. But there is no room for error. The best people in my life have still hurt me. This could all be a setup.

I look down at Enzo and I's joined hands. My husband is the only man I can trust.

17

ENZO

THERE IS an SUV waiting for us at the airport—a black Tahoe.

"Thank you, we got it from here," Beckett says to the driver, handing him cash and then climbing in the driver's seat.

I resist the urge to take over driving. If I'm not driving, then I can better protect Kai. Especially since I'm the only one with a gun.

Kai and I climb into the back seat as Beckett climbs into the front.

"What the hell are you doing, asshole?" Kai's father says before punching Beckett in the face through the driver's side window.

I grin, chuckling lightly to myself at the sight of Beckett getting punched again. He's going to have a nasty shiner tomorrow.

"Dad! Stop," Kai yells as her father drives his arm back for another swing at Beckett. But Beckett was only going to let him get one punch in any way; he's already grabbed Kai's father's arm.

"You threatened my daughter's life. I'm going to kill you."

"No, I saved your daughter's life. I warned them that Felix is coming. And I'm ensuring we all get on a yacht and get our butts out of here before Felix and his men get here," Beckett disarms Kai's father before he's even able to draw his weapon.

I don't know how Beckett was trained, but he has skills, I'll give him that.

"Beckett's on our side," Kai says.

Her father looks at her with unbelieving eyes. He turns his attention to me. And I gaze frustratingly back, conveying my forced discontent. We don't have any other option.

Kai's father tenses more at my reaction.

"Give him back the gun, Beckett," I say.

Beckett slowly hands Kai's father the gun.

He takes it, resisting the urge to knock Beckett over the head with it.

"Get in the car, Dad," Kai says.

He reluctantly climbs into the front seat, still gripping his gun. Beckett starts driving, not waiting for permission to leave.

"What the hell is going on?" Kai's dad says.

"We are getting out of here. Felix is out of prison and headed here. There is a yacht waiting for us. Trust me," Kai says.

Trust me.

The same words she said to me.

Her father has fucked up as bad or worse than I did. He can't argue with her when she says to trust him.

He nods, slowly agreeing to trust Kai.

"But keep your gun out and ready. We don't know when our enemies will attack," I say, meaning Beckett.

Beckett's shoulder's tense at my words. He's in a vulnerable position. I'm sitting behind him with a gun in my hand. Kai's father is sitting next to him with a gun. Both of us would prefer it if he were dead. And the only weapon Beckett has is the car he is driving. If he wrecks us though, he's risking his own life as well. So I have to hope Beckett wants to live to keep all of us safe.

It takes ten minutes to reach the docks. I see the shiny, black yacht towering over the other boats in the distance. It's not parked at the dock. The harbor is too shallow; instead, it is anchored in deeper water. We will have to take a dingy boat over to reach it.

Beckett parks the car between two others in the small parking lot. The tension whisks in the air. We are so close to safety, and yet so far away. We just need to get to the yacht, and then we can disappear until Kai has the babies. I'll fly an entire medical team to us to take care of her.

"We need to move quickly, but inconspicuously. We are most vulnerable here. I can't hide a yacht from Felix. If he's made it to Alaska, he will know we are here," Beckett says.

"Everyone on alert. And we protect Kai at all costs. We all stand around her and don't let a single bullet through," I say.

"Agreed," Kai's father says, glaring at Beckett.

"I agree," Beckett says.

Kai opens her mouth, ready to disagree, but then stops and rubs her stomach. She knows she has to be the one we protect—no matter what.

I get out of the car first, then Beckett and Kai's father get out. Finally, I nod for Kai to get out with me.

Kai's father and I have our weapons drawn, but by our sides, hoping no one notices us. But even if someone does and calls the police, we will be long gone before the authorities arrive.

Kai does as she's told and walks in the middle of us. Beckett leads the front, and her father and I walk on either side of her.

I can feel Kai's heart flittering quickly beside me, so I take her hand and give it a squeeze. But I don't assure her that it will be okay, because I don't know if it will be or not.

We start down the pier. I spot the dingy boat I assume we are headed toward at the very end. We continue to walk, and I don't spot any men that seem suspicious—not one man who has worked for me in the past. Most men seem to be in their fifties or older. Not fit men ready to attack us.

"This doesn't feel right," I say.

"I agree. Even if Felix didn't make it here in time, we should face some opposition here from his men. At the very least his men should be trailing us so Felix can follow us later. But I don't see anyone—" Beckett never gets to finish his words.

An explosion rings out behind us, decimating half the pier.

"Run!" I yell, knowing the only way we make it out of here is to get into the water. I don't even trust the dingy boat.

We all start sprinting, but Kai can't sprint fast enough to outrun the chain of explosions firing faster and faster behind us.

I scoop her up in my arms and start running as I toss my gun to Beckett.

He turns to fire behind us, but there are no men to fire at. The entire pier is rigged with explosives. The men aren't here. They are waiting elsewhere, hoping the explosives do the job.

"We need to get into the water," Beckett shouts.

I nod, agreeing. But there are boats lining each side of the pier. It's impossible to get off without running off the end.

I run as fast and as hard as I can while carrying Kai and my babies in her belly. My entire future rests in my hands and how fast I can run. I've never run so fast in my life, but that doesn't mean I can outrun fate.

I feel the blast before it hits me, and I know I failed, even though I'm running faster than Beckett or Kai's father. It's still not fast enough. We are only ten feet from the end of the pier. So close to safety. But still so far away.

We are falling, the blast knocking us sideways. And I do everything I can as we fly through the air to be the one who hits the ground first instead of Kai or the babies. Somehow the world hasn't completely turned on us, and I cushion Kai's fall. My shoulder taking the brunt of the blow as we are knocked to the ground.

"Run!" I yell to Kai. We can't stop.

She gets up and holds out her hand.

"Run!" I yell, telling her with one word that I'm coming, but she has to go now. She has to save our babies, our future. She has to put herself first.

I see the pain, but in a split second, she starts running.

I see the next explosive. If I can dismantle it, I'll give Kai more time to get to safety. Kai is five feet from the end of the pier. My leg is splitting, and my shoulder throbs, but I push that all out as I crawl to the side and quickly dismantle the next explosive. Giving Kai three to five more seconds to get to safety.

I scramble up to my feet to run after.

Kai's father is slightly ahead of me.

Beckett is ahead of him.

And Kai is the furthest down the pier, but her breathing

is slow and heavy. If she doesn't move faster, she won't make it.

I spot the next bomb about to go off. We are all too close to it. This one is going to impact us. But I'm not close enough to stop it.

Kai's father is. And he gives me one look—a look begging me to take care of his daughter. And then he dives onto the device.

It explodes, knocking me on my ass. I scramble back to my feet quickly. Kai's father is gone. But he contained the bomb enough that it didn't obliterate more of the pier.

I spot Beckett scrambling to his feet, while Kai is still knocked on the ground. But she's moving. She's alive. Her father just saved her life, by sacrificing his. She hasn't realized it yet. She just lost another person who loved her. And by the end of this, she might be the only one of us that survives. But her life is all that matters.

Each bomb was placed less than ten feet apart, which means there is one more. We aren't safe yet.

I run harder as I yell, "Run!" to Kai. She's barely on her feet, now seven feet from the end, the explosion knocking her back.

Beckett looks from me to Kai, making a split-second decision similar to Kai's father. He is the only one who can save Kai.

I can't.

I'm too far away.

He's close enough to grab her and get her in the water.

I won't make it. Not unless a miracle happens and the bomb doesn't go off.

Take care of her, I mouth.

Beckett grits his teeth, but instead of running toward Kai, he runs toward the bomb. He's going to try the same move that Kai's father did. Even though he knows how that ended—with his death.

It's in that moment, that I know Kai is right, Beckett is one of the good guys. He could have run off the end of the pier and gotten into the water. He could have saved himself.

Instead, he's sacrificing himself to give Kai and I a chance.

I sprint harder, ensuring his sacrifice isn't in vain.

I reach the end just as Kai jumps. I jump with her, our hands reaching out as we fall into the water. I feel the blow of the bomb, but it's not as strong as it should be. Beckett got to it in time. The only reason Kai and I are both alive is because of him.

The water welcomes us in, and I know we are safe. I should be relieved we survived it. Instead, my heart throbs for the loss of family. When we surface, we will have to face that loss. Kai lost a father, who in the end, proved that he loved his daughter in the worst possible way and paid the ultimate price to protect her.

I lost a brother, my only chance at family left to show that the blood that runs through the Black family's veins isn't evil, but good. I thought Beckett was one of the bad ones. I thought he was as broken as my half-brothers, but he proved to be a knight willing to give his own life so Kai and I could have a chance at a normal life.

The loss is going to hurt. My heart is already bleeding for his sacrifice. I didn't even know his first name. I didn't get to tell him he was my brother, even if on some level, he had suspected it himself. Now he's gone, and I can never repay his sacrifice.

Kai's hand finds me in the water, and we both start kicking for the surface. All I can do now is to continue to protect the woman he gave everything for.

18

KAI

WE CRACK the surface of the water. And take a deep breath together. We are alive. I don't fucking know how. Each detonation brought us all one step closer to death, but somehow, we made it to the water.

I know we aren't completely safe. Felix could have men in the water ready to chase after us. But from those explosions, I don't think Felix figured any of us would survive.

Enzo immediately grabs me in his arms as we both tread water. His hands run over what he can of my body, checking for injuries. But I don't feel hurt; I doubt I even have a scratch on me.

"You okay?" he asks, his voice breaking.

"Yes, I'm fine."

He puts his hands over my stomach. "The babies?"

They both kick, answering for me.

He exhales some of the pain etched on his face. But it doesn't all dissipate.

"We need to get to the yacht," he says.

I nod, knowing it's going to be difficult for me to swim that far this pregnant and exhausted.

Enzo looks torn as he notices parts of the dock floating behind us. He knows I'll need some help swimming, but he doesn't want to leave me a single second.

"Go," I say.

He wants to argue, but he really doesn't have a choice. He nods, then dives under the water so he can swim as fast as possible toward a piece of the dock I can hold onto while we swim to the yacht.

I take a deep breath looking for signs of Beckett or my father, but I see none. *Did the blast send them farther into the ocean? Are they staying afloat somewhere in the wreckage behind me?*

I spot Enzo swimming back with what looks like a buoy.

"Here, hold onto this, and I'll pull you," he says, pushing the buoy out in front of me.

I grab onto it with my arms, realizing how exhausted I am for the first time as I get some relief.

Enzo starts swimming, and I know he won't wait for my father or Beckett to catch up.

"Did you see any sign of Beckett or my father?" I ask.

Enzo is silent; he just starts swimming. *Did he not hear me?*

"Enzo?" I ask, after he swims for a minute without talking to me.

"They didn't make it," he says, after another moment passes.

I stop kicking, and the ocean seems to still as I take that in. *My father's gone. Beckett is gone.*

"How do you know?" I ask. Maybe Enzo's wrong. There is a lot of wreckage from those explosions. We can barely see five feet in front of us between the smoke, high waves, and pieces of wreckage we are swimming through.

"Because I saw it happen, both times."

"How?"

"Your father jumped on one of the explosions, dimming its strength. And Beckett," his voice breaks. "He jumped on the last one. They saved us. Without their sacrifices, we wouldn't be here. Or at least, I wouldn't."

I break. I'm used to the feeling, but this time it's different. Before I lost people I was sure I loved. People who knew I loved them. This time I lost two people who I didn't know for sure where their loyalties lied.

"My father loved me," I say, my heart thudding softly in my chest. I wasn't sure before now. But I know it's true. My uncle was my father in every way that mattered. He fucked up a lot, but in the end, he made it right. He protected me.

"There isn't any other word to describe what your father did except love. He gave up everything to keep you safe."

I close my eyes as the tears burn. Enzo continues to swim, pulling me closer to the ship. Later I will fully mourn my father's death. It will fully hit me, but right now, it doesn't.

"Why did Beckett save us?" I ask, confused. Sure, I thought he was on our side, but not enough to sacrifice himself to save us. Enzo must have gotten that part wrong.

"Because you were right. He's a good guy." Enzo pauses, then corrects himself as he stops swimming. "He was a good guy. And he saw that our love was worth dying for."

Enzo's pain is palpable. I can feel it from here, even though I'm not touching him.

"It's not your fault that Beckett's dead. It's not your fault that you never knew he existed. That you never had a chance to grow up as brothers," I say, but I know the words don't mean much to him.

He doesn't say anything as he continues to swim. The smoke has somehow gotten thicker as we swim further out. Enzo dodges pieces of ships and wooden chunks from the pier as we swim.

But a soft groan perks my ears up. "Did you hear that?"

"No."

But the man moans again, making the sound undeniable.

"We have to help him," I say as I hear the sound a third time to my left.

"Kai, we can't. We need to get to the yacht. We can't have stowaways on the ship. It's not safe."

"Just stop, please," I say, something drawing me to the sound of the man groaning.

Enzo stops, and we start moving left toward the sound of a man dying. *Please let us be able to save him.* Whoever he is, I need something positive right now after learning of too much death.

The smoke lifts just enough to make out the man, he's draped over a piece of wood floating in the water. He looks burned and covered in brown splotches of soot. His arm looks battered; I can see the muscles, veins, and arteries. But his eyes open, and my mouth drops. "Beckett?"

Enzo freezes for a just a second, and then he swims hard and fast toward the man clinging to life a few feet away. I want to go to him, but decide it's better to hold onto the buoy than let go and swim to him.

"It's Beckett!" Enzo shouts back.

Enzo grabs the piece of wood serving as a life raft and swims furiously back to me.

"We need to get him to the yacht, fast. He's barely hanging on," Enzo says.

If it wasn't for the constant moans, I would think Beckett is already dead.

"I'm going to put him on the buoy with you and then swim as hard as I can to the yacht," Enzo says.

I nod.

I move to the far edge as Enzo drapes Beckett's body over the buoy. Then I put my arm over Beckett, to help hold him to the buoy. Enzo starts swimming hard, and I kick as best I can as we swim full-on toward the yacht in the distance.

"Hold on, Beckett. Just a little longer," I whisper to him over and over. If not for me, then for Enzo. He needs him to live. He can't have anyone else sacrifice for him. He can't lose anyone else because they put his life over theirs.

Beckett's eyes finally open through the swelling and redness.

"We got you, just hold on," I say.

He blinks but doesn't say anything. But he's alive; he's breathing, that's all that matters.

I've never seen Enzo swim so hard in his life. He looks like a dolphin in the water; nothing will slow him down. Not the waves, muscle fatigue, or exhaustion. Beckett is complete dead weight, and I'm barely kicking. Enzo is doing all of the work. And he's doing it better than if we were all healthy and swimming along next to him.

Enzo has always been at home in the water, the same as me. But it isn't until now that I realize just how at home he is. How much the only time the universe is on our side is when we are both on the water.

Enzo kicks it into another gear. He doesn't look back at us. He doesn't try to talk to me. He just swims with every ounce of energy he has.

And somehow we make it to the yacht with Beckett still alive. If anything, Beckett seems more alert now than he was before.

Enzo grabs onto the ladder at the back of the yacht. He's panting hard, exhaling oxygen as he sucks it in.

I realize Enzo is too out of breath to talk.

"You lift Beckett, and I'll push," I say.

Enzo nods, grabbing Beckett under the arms, while I use what strength I have to push. Enzo ends up doing most of the work as he pulls Beckett up onto the yacht. I climb up the ladder afterward.

When I hit the deck, the sight scares me a little. Both Enzo and Beckett are spread out on the floor. Both breathing heavily like they just finished a marathon. And I don't know what to do to help either of them.

"Get...us...out..." Enzo says between heavy pants looking up at me.

Enzo didn't finish his words, but I know what he wants. For me to get us the hell out of here. We can't handle an attack right now.

I glance down at Beckett, who is bleeding heavily from somewhere out onto the deck. And Enzo looks more beat up and in pain than I realized in the water. I want to help them. But I can't help them until I get us away, somewhere safe.

"Go," Enzo says between more strained breathing.

I close my eyes trying to gather strength to leave, and hoping that when I return, Beckett will still be alive. Because I can't watch the heartbreak Enzo will go through thinking he wasn't enough to save Beckett.

I run, even though I'm physically exhausted. I grip my stomach, praying I'm not doing anything to hurt my babies.

But all I can remember is my OBGYN saying exercise is good for the babies. So running can't be bad.

I make it to the bridge, trying my best to not think about the fact that Felix or his men could already be on this ship. This could all be a trap. Another explosion could go off and ring through all of us, destroying all of the work we did to stay alive.

But there is nothing I can do about that. If Felix is here, then we are all dead. But if he is out there, in the water or still in town, then I still have time to do something. I can get us out of here, help us disappear.

I stand, looking at all the controls. I've watched Enzo and others drive the yachts we've been on before, but why did I never ask to be taught how to work one?

I close my eyes, trying to remember the last image of Enzo driving a yacht. I try to remember his motions.

Press the button to bring the anchor up. It was over on the right. I look to the right, try a button, and hear the anchor going up.

"Okay, I got this," I say to myself.

Now, I need to turn on the engines. I stare at the panel. It takes me three tries before I get it right.

Power—that one's easier. I push on the lever. And we are moving.

I exhale, *thank god.*

I speed up, knowing we need to get as far away from here as fast as possible.

I grip the helm and drive us as far away from land as I can.

I don't know how much time passes. *Ten minutes? Twenty? Thirty?*

We aren't safe. I know that. But it's the best I can do at the moment. I can no longer see land. And it will take Felix and his men a while to find us. I turn off the engine but decide not to put the anchor down. I hope we continue to float away from the shore, making it harder for Felix to find us.

And then I run back to the men who saved me and my babies' lives.

They are both sitting up, which I take as a good sign.

Enzo looks at me like I'm his whole world, and he couldn't function with me gone. Now that I've returned, he's whole again. I smile lightly; I feel the exact same way.

And then I look at Beckett. He looks like he just went through a meat grinder. I don't see a spot of skin that isn't burned or marked. His left eye is bulging out of his eye socket swollen and red. And his right arm looks the worst. It must have taken the brunt of the damage from the explosion. It's bleeding badly as he cradles it against his chest. I can see the muscles and tendons exposed where skin should be. Blood is shooting rapidly from his veins. If we don't do something, he's going to bleed to death.

"I should have driven us to a hospital instead of getting lost," I say, realizing my mistake as I look at Beckett.

"No," Enzo and Beckett both say at the same time.

"I don't need a doctor," Beckett says.

"Well, you can't keep walking around like that," I say, but inside I'm thrilled Beckett is at least conscious enough to talk again, although he must be in incredible pain.

"He needs surgery," Enzo says.

My eyes widen, looking at Beckett's arm. I don't disagree. But neither Enzo or I can perform a surgery.

"Did you call a doctor to meet us here?" I ask.

Enzo looks at Beckett. "Do you trust me?"

Beckett stares back. "With my life."

Enzo stands, his energy seeming to return. Then he

walks over to Beckett. He kneels down so Beckett can put his better arm around Enzo's shoulder, and Enzo helps Beckett stand.

"Kai, there should be a medical room on the yacht. Most often it's the first room on the right down the first flight of stairs."

I nod and disappear down the stairs.

Sure enough, Enzo is right. There is a room set up to handle a medical crisis on board. It looks similar to the room Enzo had set up in his house. I prop the door open so Enzo and Beckett can easily get through, and then I dig through cabinets trying to find all the supplies we will need to help Beckett.

I find gauze, bandages, morphine, needles, and then I see a saw. I hold it in my hand a second, considering, but we can't do that. I move to put it back in the cabinet.

"We are going to need that," Beckett says before I can put the saw away.

I swallow hard, not able to imagine using it to remove Beckett's arm. Even if we were successful in numbing his arm and knocking him unconscious, I don't think we can amputate it. But I also don't think we can repair the damage.

So I set the saw on the tray next to the surgery table.

Enzo helps Beckett to the table and remove his shirt. Beckett hisses as he has to lift his mangled arm.

I stare at Beckett's body, broken and marred. All of my own scars flare at the sight, bringing back all the pain I've experienced before. But I've never felt anything like his arm.

I know staring at it isn't helping, but I don't know what to do.

"We need to deal with your arm first. We don't want you to bleed out on us," Enzo says.

Beckett nods.

I tense, trying not to cry. "If he needs blood, I can give him some." We learned after Enzo needed blood that since I'm O negative, I can give blood to anyone. It doesn't matter their blood type.

"No," Beckett says. "I won't put you or the babies at risk."

I stroke his face. "I don't think giving a little of my blood would be putting me or the babies at risk."

Beckett frowns though, not liking it. "Let's get through the worst part first; then we will see if I need blood."

"What's your blood type?" Enzo asks.

"A negative," Beckett says.

"I can give him blood. I'm the same blood type," Enzo says.

My eyes flicker back and forth between the two men. Still, neither of them has admitted out loud that they know the other is his brother. Now probably isn't the best time.

"I'm going to give you some morphine to help with the pain," Enzo says.

Beckett nods and doesn't even flinch as Enzo inserts the needle into his arm and pushes the drug in.

"The drug will probably take a few minutes to kick in, but..." Enzo can't finish his sentence.

Beckett chuckles. "But you can't wait, or I'll bleed out and die. I know. Don't act like you aren't going to enjoy this." Beckett picks up the saw and hands it to Enzo.

I can't hide my horror. I know if we leave Beckett's arm attached he will bleed out and die. Or it will get infected, and he'll die slowly, even if we can stop the bleeding. I'm not sure how amputating his arm will reduce the blood loss, but I know his arm either needs a very skilled surgeon to try and stitch it back together, or it needs to be amputated. But I can't imagine the pain he will feel. And not just the physical pain, the emotional loss of an arm.

Enzo grabs a tourniquet and wraps it around the undamaged upper part of Beckett's arm.

I can't watch. I'm not strong enough.

But I can't leave. I'm not selfish enough.

"What would the woman of your dreams do in a situation like this?" I ask Beckett, mirroring how he behaved when I was in the hospital, and Enzo wasn't there.

"She'd flash me her boobs and give me a lap dance."

I laugh, and we both look up at Enzo, who is barely keeping his anger under control. He's stiff, red, and practically chewing his bottom lip off.

I smirk at Beckett, knowing he just said that to get a rise out of Enzo. But to Enzo's credit, he doesn't say anything to Beckett.

"Seriously, though?" I ask, needing to be here for Beckett. He is my brother-in-law, after all. And he risked his life to save mine and Enzo's. I owe him everything.

He sighs. "Hold my hand. Tell me how much she loves me. Distract me."

I nod and grab the hand that isn't about to get chopped off as I stroke his face.

"Are you sure?" Enzo asks, his voice strong and steady. There is no hesitation or resistance. He's strong enough to do this.

If it were Beckett's life rested in my hands and required being able to drive the saw into his arm, I don't think I could do it.

"Get it over with, man," Beckett says.

I grab Beckett's head and turn it toward me and away from Enzo, while I silently pray the morphine or adrenaline has kicked in, and Beckett won't feel this.

Enzo drives the saw into his arm, and the scream from

Beckett is something I've never heard before. It's guttural, torturous, and all consuming.

I wince and blink back my tears as Beckett continues to scream and twist his head, but tries to remain still on the table.

I grab Beckett's head again and turn him toward me. Doing what he asked of doing what the love of his life would do if she were here.

"I love you, Beckett. You are so strong. You saved my life. You saved Enzo's life. You saved my future. I can never repay you."

He calms a little as I speak. But tears run down his face in floods. And I know every time Enzo goes to work again, because Beckett's screams return.

"Do you hear me, Beckett? You are so loved. I owe you everything. And I'll spend my life trying to pay you back. You are so loved," I say, but Beckett's screaming gets worse.

"Kiss him," Enzo says suddenly.

"What?" I ask, so confused.

"Kiss him," Enzo growls.

The situation is so intense. But I grab Beckett's lips and kiss him hard on the lips. Beckett doesn't know how to respond. His lips don't part. He doesn't welcome me in with his tongue like Enzo would. Our lips are just pressed together. But Beckett is no longer screaming in pain. I don't know if it's the shock of the kiss that halted the screaming or if he can't get enough oxygen to scream. Or maybe the endorphins from the kiss are helping with the pain. Whatever it is, it seems to help. So I keep my lips pressed against his.

"You can stop, stingray," I hear Enzo's weak voice.

I lift my lips and realize that Beckett has passed out.

I look up at Enzo. Both of us have tear-stained eyes.

"You wanted me to kiss him so he would pass out?" I ask.

Enzo's eyes water more. "Yes, I thought if you made it harder for him to breathe, he would pass out on his own. The drugs were taking too long to kick in, and if I gave him more, I could kill him. But I thought depriving him of oxygen for a few minutes would calm his system down enough to go unconscious."

"But I could have just covered his mouth and nose for a few seconds; I didn't have to kiss him."

Enzo tucks a strand of my hair behind my ear. "That seemed too cruel. This seemed kinder."

I smile through my tears. "You are a good brother."

"Don't say that. It killed me watching you kiss him even though I knew it meant nothing."

"I know. I'm sorry."

"I need to finish."

I nod, and we fall silent as Enzo finishes sawing through tendon and bones.

When the arm is separated, he applies pressure, flushes out the wound, then stitches him up, stopping the bleeding.

But when I look on the floor under the table and see the amount of blood, I'm not sure Beckett is going to make.

"He's going to make it, he just needs my blood," Enzo says.

I nod. I race over and grab the needle and tubbing, happy to help in some way. Then I place the needle into Beckett's vein carefully before going over to Enzo. I don't like hurting him, even with a needle.

Enzo smiles. "I can handle a needle poke."

I nod. "Right, sorry." I wipe my face and then insert the needle into his arm as I'd watch the doctor do before when I was giving blood to Enzo.

I watch carefully, not able to breathe until I see the blood flowing from Enzo to Beckett.

Now, all we can do is wait, and pray that Beckett wakes up. We've done everything we can for him. He just has to find a way back—a way to wake up. Beckett has to choose to live.

19

ENZO

WAITING SUCKS.

I fucking hate waiting. But that's what we've been doing for hours—waiting.

Kai and I have taken turns cruising the yacht further out to sea. Zigging and zagging our path, hoping Felix won't be able to find us. We both secretly wish we could stay right next to Beckett's side and wait for him to wake up.

Beckett is strong. I know that. There is no way he should have survived the explosion. He shouldn't have survived floating in the water. He shouldn't have survived the amputation. But he did.

Now we just have to wait for him to wake up.

"You should eat," I say to Kai, who is sitting in a chair next to Beckett's bed while I pace.

"Yea, I will."

I would offer to go make her food, but I hate leaving Beckett's side. This is my fault. If he had just tried to save Kai, they would both be alive and healthy, while I would be dead or at least severely injured. It should be the other way around. I should be in Beckett's position, and him in mine.

But he saved my life. And now I can't leave his fucking side.

"Enzo," Kai says cautiously, looking at Beckett.

I race to the other side of the bed as Beckett opens his eyes.

"How are you feeling?" Kai asks.

"Like you have one deadly kiss there, woman. Your kiss was so strong you knocked me out," Beckett teases.

Kai grins. "Sorry about that, but glad to see you still have your humor. I didn't think you would remember that kiss."

"I would never forget a kiss like that," Beckett says, winking at her. But I know he's teasing me as much as reassuring her.

This time, I don't care. I don't get angry or jealous. I don't even tense up. I'm just happy he's fucking alive to rib me like this.

"And you, we need to work on your sawing skills. If it were me, I could have had your arm off in five seconds flat."

I smile.

"I'll hold you to that if I'm ever in a situation that calls for needing my arm sawed off. But unlike you, I won't do something stupid like jump on a bomb about to explode."

He grins. "Next time you are about to die from a bomb, I promise I won't jump on it."

"Good."

Kai looks from me to Beckett. "I'm going to go fix you some tea and food."

"Think you could make it something stronger than tea?" Beckett asks.

Kai smiles and nods then leaves Beckett and me alone.

"Thank you," we both say at the same time.

Beckett is silent, letting me talk first.

"Thank you for saving my life. You shouldn't have. You could have just saved Kai. I owe you everything," I say, holding the tears back but just barely. It probably helps that I've spent the last two days crying so I have nothing left.

"You would have done the same for me."

I nod. "I will do the same thing for you." I wouldn't have before, but I would now.

Beckett stares at the nub left of his arm. "Thank you for saving my life. Not many men are strong enough to saw off an arm."

"It wasn't my first time."

He grins. "I figured that. But you also didn't have to tell Kai to kiss me."

I shrug. "You needed to pass out. And I knew Kai didn't have any feelings for you. That kiss served two purposes. To get you to pass out and prove to you that Kai is mine, you never stood a chance with her."

Beckett raises an eyebrow. "I never tried to have a chance with her. I knew from the moment I saw her with you, she would never be anyone else's but yours. I didn't need her to kiss me to know that."

I nod. "Then, why did you save us?"

"Because I care about her. I love her like a sister. And when I saw what the two of you have, I knew it deserves to be protected. The love you share is rare. I couldn't just let it fail. And I knew if I had only saved her, she would never survive without you. She was only holding on for the babies before. But once they were born, she would have struggled to survive to live. She needs you."

"There is a reason you and I share a connection. A reason Felix and Kai's father both sought you out, out of all the people with your skillset in the world," I say.

"I'd like to think I'm the only one with my skill set."

I shake my head. "When you are healthy, we will see who has more skills."

"Sure, wait until I lose an arm to challenge me," Beckett says with a broad grin, lightening the mood before I turn it serious.

"Is Beckett your first or last name?" I ask.

"Last name, why?"

"Beckett was my mother's maiden name."

"Julia Beckett?" he asks, realization on his face.

"Yes."

He swallows hard. "She put me up for adoption when I was little. I never knew her. My father was listed as Leone Rinaldi."

I nod. "He also goes by Leone Black."

Tears tickle the corner of both of our eyes. "You're my brother," I say.

"Wow," Beckett finally says after a pause. "That means Felix..."

"Is also your half-brother. Welcome to the family," I chuckle.

"Jesus, my half-brother tried to kill me," he says.

"He's tried to kill me too. I'm sure he figured it out and thought he could either turn you against me or use you as bait to get me to come to him and fight for your freedom."

Beckett frowns. "Brothers."

I nod. "Brothers."

"I always wanted a sibling growing up. I had good, caring parents when I was adopted, but they didn't want another child. That's why I joined the army and eventually, the FBI. I wanted to feel that bond with someone else. That protect others at all costs thing you only get when it comes to family."

"Our mother did the right thing giving you up. Our

father would have only turned us against each other. He would have made us fight daily to prove to him who is stronger to enter the games to become Black. We wouldn't have had the chance to be real brothers. It's better this way. Because now we can be real brothers."

"I'm the better looking one," Beckett says.

I smirk. "You wish."

Beckett is blonde, with fair skin, and a big heart. He's light where I'm dark. But watching him, I realize just because you were born into the Black family doesn't mean you are destined to be bad. You can fight to live in the light. Beckett is proof of that.

"So what's your first name?" I ask.

"Eli."

I hold out my left hand. He takes it with his left hand. "It's nice to meet you, Eli."

"You too, brother. Does this mean you no longer think I'm working with Felix?'

I laugh. "Yes, Kai was right. You are on our side. One of the good ones. I trust you with my life."

"Good, I trust you with my life too."

I nod. "Sorry about your arm, though."

He shrugs. "Chicks will dig the saving my pregnant sister's life story."

"They probably will."

His smile drops. "Speaking of my sister-in-law, what are we going to do to protect her?"

I sigh and run my hand through my hair. "Everything we can."

He nods.

"We are going to sail away, never staying in one place to make it impossible for Felix to find us. We will fly a doctor out when she gives birth. And then once she and the babies are stable, we will hide them away with someone I trust to protect them. And you and I will go kill our half-brother and every other man that follows him. You and I will end this together."

Beckett grins. "Good, because I'm ready for a fight."

20

KAI

BECKETT'S RECOVERY is both easy and hard. He never once loses his humor throughout the entire process, which helps keep the emotional toll of losing his arm from overpowering him. But physically, his journey isn't easy, especially when recovering without medical help and limited drugs to help him deal with the pain.

It also doesn't help that every day we spend on the sea running from Felix is another day of anxiety, worrying he will eventually find us. The fear creeps in every day. But every day we outrun it.

I spot Beckett sitting on the edge of his bed, trying to tie his black boots. He tries again and again and then grabs the shoe off his foot and throws it at the door, barely missing hitting me.

So maybe he isn't dealing with the loss of his arm so well after all.

"Sorry, I wasn't aiming for you," he says, hanging his head between his legs.

"At least you were able to zip and button your jeans today," I say, hoping it will make him smile.

"Yep, sign me up for the Olympics, today I buttoned my own pants!"

I laugh, but I can feel the sadness in his eyes. I pick up the shoe he tossed and give it back to him.

"You want to talk about it?" I ask.

He shrugs. "There is nothing to talk about. I don't regret what I did. I would do it a thousand times over. It just sucks. You never knew how much you depend on something until it's gone."

I sit on the edge of the bed next to him. "I understand. I felt the same way after Enzo was taken from me. I always knew I loved him, but not how much it would impact my life until he was gone. I know it's not the same thing. The pain you must be experiencing is..."

He wraps his arm around me. "The pain is worth it. Every time I see you and Enzo together, I'm reminded just how worth it is. And I didn't just do it for you. I got a brother and sister out of the deal. Giving up an arm seems like a small sacrifice in comparison."

I lean my head against his chest. "I understand. I would give up an arm for you too."

He kisses the top of my head. "I know you would, but I'm glad you don't have to."

I wipe a small tear away that had fallen from my eye. Then I sit up. "But enough of the pity party. You are healing every day. I'm here to help you get stronger and make sure you can tie your own damn shoes. I'm getting too big to tie your shoes for you." I lean down to try to tie his shoes, but my oversized stomach gets in the way.

He laughs, watching me struggle. He lifts his other shoe off and hands it to me.

"Thanks," I say.

"I can't believe you still have another month left. I don't know how you are going to manage walking much longer."

I give him a dirty look. "You're not helping. I'm going to leave you to figure out how to tie your own damn shoes if you comment one more time about looking like I'm ready to pop."

He chuckles, but I'm not really upset even though I give him a dirty look. He of all people is allowed to make fun of the size of my belly. He gave an arm to make sure I'm still here.

"Anyway, back to shoe tying. I did some research and figured out how to tie a shoe with one hand. First, you cross the laces; then you use your foot to hold tension on one of the laces while your hand makes a loop with the other. Then you push that loop under the other lace. Let go of that lace with your foot. Use your fingers to wrap the lace around the loop and push it through with your thumb." I demonstrate on my lap, pretending my second hand is my foot since I can't bend over right now. I mess up three times before I finally get it right.

"Can't I just get elastic or velcro? I think that would be easier."

I laugh. "You can, but then you are guaranteeing to never date again."

"Fine," he rolls his eyes and takes the shoe from me. He ties it easily in one try.

"See! You're a fast learner!"

"What's next? Learning how to write my name? Type one-handed?" Beckett jokes.

"How about shooting a gun?" Enzo says from the doorway. "I think it's time you prove you are a better shot and stronger than me." Enzo winks at me as he crosses his arms and taunts Beckett with a challenge.

Beckett stands, "You're on."

We all head out to the top deck of the yacht. There is no one around for miles. We are currently floating several miles off the coast of Hawaii. We should be further away from land, but I think both of the boys are worried I might go into labor at any second and they will need to fly a doctor out quickly, so we don't stray too far from land.

"How about a competition to make this more interesting?" Enzo asks, knowing Beckett is tired of us both babying him. For the first week, we kept him in bed, brought him food, and hand-fed him. The second week we allowed him out of bed, but he was weak and needed help with everything from bathing to getting dressed. And even now, the simplest of things are tricky. He was right-handed. He didn't just lose an arm; he lost the arm he was used to doing everything with.

"What do you have in mind?"

"Best of five different games?"

"And what does the winner get?"

"If I win, you have to tell everyone I'm better than you," Enzo says.

"Fine, but if I win, I get to name one of your children."

Enzo looks at me as if asking permission for this arrangement to happen. I have complete faith Enzo will win. And even if he doesn't, I have no problem with Beckett naming one of our children. Enzo and I have already been trying to figure out how to honor all those that have sacrificed everything for us. And Beckett definitely makes that list.

"Deal," Enzo says.

The two shake hands. Enzo is getting better at remembering to extend his left hand when giving him a handshake or hug.

"So how are we going to make the competition fair?" Beckett asks.

Enzo turns to me. "Kai will decide each round and how you win."

Beckett rolls his eyes. "Well, I'm going to lose."

I laugh. "I don't know. Enzo cut me off from drinking any caffeine and from eating sugar, or anything bad at all. So I'm not very happy with him at the moment."

"Well, I will happily sneak you a coffee and a donut if you help me win," Beckett says, winking at me.

"Hey, none of that. Those are my babies too, and I want them happy and healthy, not addicted to sugar," Enzo says.

Beckett and I both roll our eyes. But I do secretly love how protective Enzo is of our children and how much he wants them to be healthy. I truly have no desire to eat or drink anything bad anymore.

"So what is the first game?" Beckett asks.

I know the point of this is to figure out Beckett's strengths and weaknesses and to help him feel physically ready to battle Felix after the babies are born, but I also want to tease my husband.

"First game is Kai trivia," I say.

Both men grin. They both think they know random trivia about me better than the other. But I know for a fact Beckett will win. For one, we've spent more normal time together than I have with Enzo. He knows my favorite flavors of ice cream. My favorite movie and books to read. My favorite place to sit and watch the day go by. Enzo and I have spent most of our life running or fighting danger. And I want Beckett to know he has a place in our life. And I want to tease my husband with the fact that Beckett knows silly things about me that he doesn't.

"First to three points wins. First question: what is my favorite flavor of ice cream?" I ask.

"Chocolate," Enzo answers.

"Chocolate chip cookie dough," Beckett says.

"First point goes to Beckett."

Enzo frowns, giving me a dirty glare, knowing I'm giving him no chance of winning this first game.

"That's not fair," Enzo says.

Beckett holds up his stub. "That's not fair?"

Enzo rolls his eyes and teases. "Are you going to play the *I don't have an arm* card the rest of your life?"

"Yep, I am," Beckett grins.

I grin, too.

Even Enzo smiles a little. All of us are happy that Beckett can joke about it.

"Fine, next question," Enzo says.

"What is my favorite movie?"

"Pretty Woman," Enzo says.

Beckett rolls his eyes. "Really? You think the movie with the prostitute and the guy with gray hair is your wife's favorite movie?"

"Isn't it every woman's favorite movie?" Enzo answers.

"Your wife is not most women. Your wife is more of a Katniss fan. Her favorite movie is the Hunger Games. The second in the trilogy, if we are being picky."

"Ding, ding, ding! We have a winner!" I point to Beckett.

Enzo huffs. "How about you ask an important fact, like your favorite sexual position or favorite place to be kissed?"

"Eww," Beckett covers his ears.

Enzo and I laugh.

Enzo mouths *rough missionary and pussy*—answers for favorite position and place to be kissed.

I blush and forgive my husband for not knowing my

favorite ice cream flavor or movie. He knows the important things. But I ask one more question Beckett will know the answer to and Enzo won't.

"When is the twins' due date?" I ask.

Enzo's face drops. He knows the babies are due in a month. But he doesn't know the exact date. He's never gone to a doctor's appointment with me, and he's never asked.

Beckett grins while waiting for Enzo to guess.

"October first?" Enzo guesses.

Beckett shakes his head. "September twenty-fifth."

Enzo throws up his hands. "Fine, you win. Next game is mine though."

Beckett slaps Enzo on the back. "Don't be a sore loser."

Enzo growls.

I grin, watching the two of them banter back and forth. I know they both wish they had gotten to grow up as actual brothers. Enzo grew up with Langston and Zeke as brothers. But I know it would have been different to have an ally living under the same roof.

Even if Beckett would have turned out differently. Even if he became more sinister and serious like Enzo instead of lighthearted and relaxed like he currently is, I know they both would have enjoyed that. I grip my stomach. I can't wait to see what life will be like for our twins.

"What is round two?" Enzo says, needing a win.

I decide I can't mess with them anymore, and I need to actually test Beckett's abilities for all of our sakes.

I grab a bucket of empty beer cans and set ten up in a row on the railing.

"First one to shoot five wins. And you have to start with an unloaded gun," I say, knowing I'm pushing Beckett, but he needs to be pushed. I know Enzo has plans to fight Felix after the birth. And I want to ensure Beckett is ready if he decides to join him.

Enzo hands Beckett a gun and a box of bullets. Beckett sets the box down on the table. Enzo leaves his own gun in his pants, but takes a couple of bullets from the box and lays them on the table in front of him.

"Go!" I shout.

Enzo is calm and relaxed as he takes the bullets and carefully loads his gun.

Beckett is in a frenzy. He's trying to move quickly to make up time, which only makes him go slower.

Enzo rattles off five shots before Beckett even gets his gun loaded.

Beckett frowns.

"Again," he says.

Enzo nods and puts his gun on the table.

Beckett does the same.

"Go!" I shout again, after setting up five new cans for Enzo.

This time Beckett gets his gun loaded before Enzo gets off his shots.

"Again," Beckett says, more determined.

I line the cans up again. "Go."

Beckett takes a deep breath and then matches Enzo's speed loading the bullets.

I grin. *Maybe he can do this with some practice.*

They both start firing at the same time. Enzo hits his five cans, Beckett only hits one.

"If I knew you weren't any better of a shot than Kai, then I wouldn't have offered to compete against you," Enzo jokes.

"Hey! I'm a better shot than you. My turn," I say, getting up and walking over to take the gun from Enzo.

Beckett grins, thinking he can beat me. Enzo lines up the cans and shouts at us to start.

I load the gun and fire off my shots in record time, making sure to hit Beckett's five cans too just to prove I'm better than either of the boys.

"Wow, if I'd had known you could shoot like that I wouldn't have offered my protection skills. I would have just handed you a gun and sat back and watched," Beckett says.

I grin. "I learned from the best." My heart aches thinking of Zeke and Langston.

Enzo frowns. "That's enough shooting from you. At least until September twenty-fifth when the babies are born. And even then, I want you in the nursery, not wielding a gun."

I roll my eyes at the sexist remark, but I know Enzo is just worried about me and the babies. I know he couldn't live with himself if I got hurt. And I have no desire to shoot a gun if I don't have to. But I'm happy I have the skillset to.

I waddle back to my chair as the men finish competing in sprints, one-handed pushups, and another shooting game.

My life is perfect at the moment, even if the reason for the game is to get Beckett ready for an inevitable fight. I don't care. I'm happy watching the two of them act like normal brothers.

And in one month our world is about to get a whole lot happier. But I feel my stomach tighten in horrible cramps, and I remember something I read off-handedly at the doctor's office—something about how twins often come early.

21

ENZO

I FEEL it the moment my world changes.

Possibly even before Kai realizes what is happening. One moment, I'm schooling Beckett on how to shoot a gun, the next my gaze is locked on Kai. I watch her stomach clench as she grabs it, her face twisting in pain.

I drop my gun on the table and run to her. I grab her face needing to see in her eyes, if she's okay. If something is wrong with the babies or not. I'm not sure she will tell me just how serious the situation is with her words. I need to see her eyes—they won't lie to me.

"Kai, what's wrong?" I ask.

She purses her lips and blows air out as another wave of pain permeates through her body.

"Kai? Baby? You need to tell me what's wrong," I say.

Another push of air through her lips. "I think...I think the babies are coming."

Shit.

They aren't supposed to come this early. She still has weeks lefts. Three and a half weeks to be exact.

I look behind her to Beckett who is standing motionless,

like he can't believe this is happening either. One minute she was fine, now she can barely stand she's in so much pain.

Beckett and I trade glances, but neither of us moves. Kai lets out a guttural growl. One sound of pain from her, and she's caused two grown men to freeze in terror.

Kai notices both of our reactions. She takes another deep breath, and then she seems to get a little more life back in her eyes. "Okay, so I think I'm in labor. We won't know for sure until my contractions are more consistent. But Beckett, it's probably a good idea to call the doctor and see if we can get someone on a helicopter to meet us."

Beckett snaps awake. "Yes, of course. I'll make the call."

"And you," Kai looks at me. "Fix me something to eat."

"To eat? You sure?"

"Yes, I'm going to need my energy if I'm going to give birth today."

I nod. "Of course!"

I race down the stairs and start pulling everything out of the fridge—eggs, spinach, carrots, chicken, cheese. Everything comes out as I start scrambling an egg while simultaneously grilling the chicken. I get so focused on the task she gave me that I forget about the most important thing—Kai.

"Kai!" I shout.

"I'm here, I'm right here," she says, walking slowly around the dining room table, swaying her hips hard back and forth as she walks.

"Jesus, you scared me."

She smiles at me. "Are you finished cooking yet?"

"No, I just got so focused on cooking that I forgot to check on you."

"That was the idea," she grins as she rubs her belly gently.

"What?"

"You need to calm down. I love you, but you are already a mess, and we haven't gotten anywhere near the hard part. I thought focusing on something that isn't me right now might help you."

I frown. "I'm calm."

She raises an eyebrow.

And I look at what she's staring at. I have oil, egg, and cheese all over the front of my shirt. I'm sweating like I just finished a workout. And my hand is trembling as I still grip the spatula in my hand.

"Fuck," I say, rubbing my neck.

She slowly walks over to me and wraps her arms around my waist. "This is a marathon, not a sprint. Go change. Then finish making us some food. Everything is going to be okay."

I kiss her forehead. "Everything is going to be okay," I repeat her words as much for her as for me.

"Go," she says.

"Are you sure? What if—"

"The babies aren't coming in the next twenty minutes. My contractions just started. Go."

Reluctantly, I go take a quick shower and shake out my nerves. When I return, she's standing in front of the stove cooking the eggs I started.

She smiles when she sees me. "Better?"

"Yes."

I walk over to her and wrap my arms around her. "I can't believe you are the one in labor, and you had to calm me down. It should be the other way around."

She laughs, leaning her head back against my chest. "I'm sure you will repay the favor soon."

We hear footsteps, and both turn around. Beckett is standing in the doorway, pale and white.

"What?" I snap. Clearly, I've not completely calmed down.

Beckett looks from me to Kai. "The doctor isn't coming."

"What?" I growl.

Beckett ignores me and looks at Kai. "There is a really bad storm between us and Hawaii. Tropical storm level. I called three different hospitals. No doctor was willing to travel through the storm to get to us." He looks to me. "I offered to pay any amount of money, but no doctor was willing to risk it."

I open my mouth to speak, but Kai puts her hand against my chest, telling me she has this.

"Is there any other island nearby? Any other way we can travel safely to a hospital?" she asks.

Beckett shakes his head. "There isn't another nearby island. I looked at the radar and weather stations. They think the storm will blow through in the next eight hours. After the brunt of the storm has passed, several doctors said they'd be willing to travel."

Kai nods slowly. "Eight hours." She touches her stomach. "We just have to make it eight hours, and then a doctor will be here. Labor, especially a first-time labor, can take days. So we have time. We will be fine. And even if the doctor doesn't make it, women all over the world give birth safely without a doctor. We got this." Her eyes travel from Beckett to me.

"We got this," we both say in return.

But I'm not sure we got this. The babies are coming early. She's having twins. And she's endured more stress during this pregnancy than most women. We are on a ship in the middle of the ocean, with a storm brewing only a few miles from us, and an evil half-brother chasing us. This is the opposite of fine.

But none of that is helpful to say to Kai.

So instead, we finish cooking the food. And then we sit at the table and try to eat. But after two bites, Kai can't stand to sit anymore. Or eat.

She gets up abruptly.

"Kai?" I ask.

"I'm sorry, I can't," she says, tears forming in her eyes.

Shit.

Both Beckett and I push our chairs back roughly as we stand abruptly.

"You can't what?" I ask.

"Do this."

Oh shit. We are only on hour one, and I've already had a breakdown, and now Kai is having one.

"Sure, you do," I say, moving over to rub her back. But apparently, I did the wrong thing, because she swats my hand away. "That doesn't help. The pain..."

She closes her eyes as another contraction hits, over-powering everything else going on in her brain.

I try rubbing her back again, and this time, she lets me.

Finally, the contraction ends, and a tear falls. I wipe it away quickly with my thumb. I can't stand to watch her in pain.

"What do you need? How can I help you? What did the books say about how to help with the pain?" I ask.

She huffs. "You think I had time to read the baby books when we were being chased by a crazy man?"

"I'm sorry." Apparently, I'm not going to say the right things.

I look to Beckett, who just shrugs like he doesn't have a clue what to do either.

"Research it," I snap at him.

He nods and grabs his laptop; he starts typing furiously while we wait for another contraction.

"Moving around can help. Don't stay in one spot. Try moving your hips and see if that helps alleviate the pain," Beckett says.

Kai starts moving around more, but then a contraction hits, and she stops moving. I walk behind her, grab her hips gently, and sway them back and forth. It seems to help because she doesn't cry or groan through this contraction. She just lets it happen.

But ten minutes later, another contraction comes, and she's cursing and crying again.

Fuck, I can't do this.

"Try positive affirmations. Don't call them a contraction. Call them a wave," Beckett yells.

"It's just a wave. Just like the tide. We like the water; the babies are going to love the water. This is just a wave helping us meet the babies," I say, trying what the internet says.

"I hate fucking waves," Kai screams through another contraction, now less than five minutes apart. We've only made it two hours so far. We have at least six more to go before we have any chance of getting a doctor here. And with how fast things seem to be speeding up, I don't feel like we have five minutes to wait, let alone six hours.

"What else does the internet say?" I ask, so far none of the techniques are working.

"Breathing, massage, pressure points, taking a bath, getting an epidural," Beckett says.

"Yes, I want the epidural," Kai says.

Beckett and I both laugh.

Somehow Kai and I ended up sitting on the floor of the

kitchen, my legs are spread, and she is sitting between them resting against my chest.

"I'm sorry, baby. I wish I could get you the epidural."

She sighs. "I know, it's not your fault. It's probably better for the babies not to get one anyway."

I kiss her cheek. "You're strong. The strongest I know."

"Let's try the tub, before another contraction hits," she says.

"Wave," both Beckett and I say in unison.

She just rolls her eyes.

Beckett races downstairs to start a bath, while I slowly help Kai stand and walk down the stairs.

We get to the small bathroom of the yacht, and I curse for not creating bigger bathrooms on this ship. The next one I build will have plenty of room in the bathroom.

"I'll just be right outside researching birth things," Becketts says, scooting past us.

I help Kai undress and get into the tub. I take off my pants, but the tub is too small for both of us, so I sit on the edge of the tub behind her, putting my feet in the tub next to her as I rub her back through each wave.

But after thirty more minutes of waves, I no longer call them waves—they are fucking contractions. They are hell. I'm happy I'm sitting behind her because she can't see how much pain I'm in watching her in pain and not being able to do anything about it.

The door opens slowly, and Beckett sticks his head in. His eyes are also puffy and red. He's been crying too. It's impossible not to while listening to Kai's deep groans, panting, and crying.

He looks at me, asking how he can help.

I shrug. I have no idea.

He stands in the doorway, staring at his watch during her contraction. "I think the babies are coming," he says.

"What? No, we still have hours left to wait until the doctor can come," I say.

He nods. "I know, but her contractions are basically on top of each other, and they are strong. Everything I read says that means it's time to start pushing."

I stroke Kai's head, but before I can respond another contraction comes. She squeezes my hand hard until I can no longer feel my fingers.

"I can't do this," she cries loudly.

"And everything I read said women almost always go through an *I can't do this* stage right before they give birth."

I frown. "She's been saying that for the last ten minutes."

"It's time."

Kai barely acknowledges either of us. She's in her own little world. But the bathroom is too small to give birth in. She needs to get into the bedroom.

I break the silence. "Kai, we are going to move to the bedroom."

She just growls and grips my hand roughly.

Beckett grabs a towel as I help her stand. I dry her off with the towel and offer her a shirt to wear, but she definitely doesn't care about modesty right now.

It takes us forever to walk the five feet to the bedroom, but finally, we make it.

"Kai, we think the babies are coming. Do you feel like pushing?" I ask.

"Yes," she screams, like that sounds like the best idea.

I help her onto the bed, hoping it's the right thing to do. *Women give birth in beds, right?*

She lays back and bends her knees, but after one

contraction in that position, Kai is completely uncom-
fortable.

"Try getting on all fours or squatting," Beckett says.

I give him a dirty look, not happy with him seeing Kai
naked or telling her to get on all fours.

He laughs, which at least relaxes the two of us a tiny bit.
Kai barely acknowledges that either of us is here. She gets
on all fours and starts pushing with the next contraction.

"Is a baby coming?" Kai moans.

"Yes, oh my god! I can see hair," I say.

I keep rubbing her back and watching for the babies,
while Beckett moves to her head, rubbing her shoulders
gently.

"Fuck, this hurts!" Kai screams.

"You got this, baby. Only a few more minutes and the
babies will be here," I say.

She looks up at Beckett and must give him a dirty look
because he looks terrified.

"What can I do? Should I kiss you like you kissed me?"
he asks, trying to get her to relax.

She moans, "Not helping, Beckett."

"Sorry, sorry."

But I catch the corner of her smile, and I know his joke
helped her just a little.

She takes a deep breath as she gets a break from the
contractions. When another contraction hits, she cries out.

"Push, baby. You have to push," I say.

Beckett rubs her back, and I prepare to catch the first
baby.

"One more push. You are so fucking strong, Kai."

She pushes, and I catch the first baby in my arms.

Suddenly, everyone goes silent. All eyes are on me as I
cradle the baby.

"Is the baby..." Kai asks, terrified to ask if the baby is alive or dead.

But then the baby cries loudly at the top of her lungs, and we all breathe in relief.

Beckett stands and grabs some scissors he brought from the medical room to me. I cut the cord. And then I hand him the baby, which he immediately wraps in a blanket and shows to Kai who strokes her little face with happy tears in her eyes.

"She's beautiful."

But then another contraction makes her focus again.

"Okay, baby. You got this. One more time," I say, amazed at how incredible my wife is.

But this time, when she pushes, the baby seems to go further up inside of her instead of coming out.

Fuck. I don't know what to do. I don't know how to help her. All I know is this isn't supposed to happen. The baby is supposed to come out, not retreat inside her. And I know if we don't get the baby out soon, that this isn't going to end well.

"Stingray, I need you to push harder. This baby needs more help than the first."

"I'm trying," Kai cries back.

I move to look her in the eyes. "Stingray, you can do this. I need you to take a deep breath and when you feel the next contraction push with everything you have."

She pushes harder than ever before, and finally, the baby descends down.

I catch the baby, and Kai collapses.

Baby number two cries immediately, and relief fills the room. I cut the second cord. And then wrap our baby boy in a blanket before helping Kai scoot back on the bed. I put our son on her chest, and Beckett puts our daughter alongside her brother.

"They are so little," she says.

"They are perfect," I say, wrapping my arms around them all.

"Congratulations, Kai. They are incredible," Beckett says.

"Thank you, truly, for everything," she says.

He nods. "I'm going to go see about getting a doctor here to check everyone over."

"Thank you," I say, choked up. I'm not sure we would have had a healthy delivery without his help and research telling us what to do.

He nods and then leaves me alone with my new family. A family I'm already willing to die for. A family I will do anything to protect.

22

KAI

"THAT ONE HAS QUITE the pair of lungs on him," the doctor says.

Enzo frowns at the doctor, not liking him to imply are our children are anything but perfect.

"Are we finished?" Enzo asks the doctor.

"Yes, everyone has a clean bill of health," the doctor says. "You all did a fantastic job considering the circumstances."

"Kai was incredible," Enzo says.

"Do you have any names picked out yet for these little ones?" the doctor asks as he packs up his things.

I look to Enzo. We both have some ideas, but we haven't decided yet. And we wouldn't be sharing the names with the doctor first.

"Not yet," I answer, holding our daughter closer against my chest.

Enzo is rocking our son in his arms who has quieted down a little but is still chirping.

"Well, I'm sure you will get it figured out soon. Please

call me if you have any other questions or concerns," the doctor says before leaving.

"I thought he'd never leave," Enzo says as he carries our son over to the bed and climbs in next to me. The baby is now quietly sleeping in his father's arms now that the doctor has left.

"He's right though; we need to decide on names," I say.

"What are you thinking?" he asks.

"I'm thinking we have a lot of people we'd like to honor when we name them."

He nods, looking solemn as he agrees with me. "I just don't think I can handle calling our son Zeke every day. It will be too hard."

"I agree. We need to honor them, not have their first name be the exact same name." I stare down at the daughter in my arms. "I'd like to name our daughter after Beckett."

"I'm not calling our daughter Beckett, or Beck," Enzo says.

I smile. "No, but how about a play on his first name, Eli? We could call her Ellie."

"Ellie, I like that," Enzo says.

I look down at my daughter, the name already fits. "Ellie Liesel Black."

Enzo nods. "It's perfect."

Baby Ellie. She has dark hair, cute chubby cheeks, and her father's eyes. But she's already a momma's girl, preferring to lay on my chest and fuss anytime her father holds her.

"So what do we think for him?" I ask.

Enzo studies our son closely. "How about Finn?"

"Finn? I like it, but how does that honor anyone?"

He grins looking at our son who is already Finn. "You

won't believe this, but Finn is both Langston and Zeke's middle name. When we were kids, I used to yell Finn whenever I wanted them both to come or fight for my attention. I just had to yell their middle names, and they would both come."

I stroke our son's cheek. "Finn, I love it."

"Finn Beckett Black. Beckett represents both Eli and my mother."

It feels right.

Enzo pauses. "What about your father, though? Your birth parents?"

"My birth parents were just a figment of my imagination. I know they existed. I know they loved me, but I never really knew them. Naming our child after one of them doesn't really feel right. And my father, he wasn't a proud guy. He wouldn't have wanted a child named after him. He would have said it's foolish to name a child after him. And plus, I'll carry my father with me everywhere; I don't need a name to remember him."

"Ellie and Finn," Enzo says, testing the names together.

Both babies look up at him with big eyes. They both seem happy with the names.

Finn coos softly, being the more vocal one of the pair. He has light blonde hair, closer to Beckett in color than Enzo's dark. But his eyes match my blue-green.

Holding both babies, and seeing the connection Enzo has to them; I have no doubt they belong to us. Milo doesn't even enter the picture.

"My perfect family," Enzo says, kissing each of us. "All mine."

His words mirror my thoughts.

Enzo grabs his phone and calls Beckett to come in here.

"You rang, oh, master?" Beckett enters and does a little bow like he's our servant or something.

I laugh.

Enzo rolls his eyes.

"What can I do to serve you, master? Would you like a scrumptious meal? For me to fill a bath? Does young master need a diaper change?"

I keep laughing.

"Shut up and come here, you oaf. I'm glad we didn't grow up together, or I would have killed you. Your jokes suck, man," Enzo says.

"My jokes are awesome," Beckett says, walking over to stare down at the babies. "How are my niece and nephew doing?" He grins at them then looks up at us. "You really need to name them; I'm tired of calling them, my niece and nephew."

I laugh. "That's why you are here."

"Even though you didn't win against me, we thought we would include you a little in the naming process," Enzo says.

"You're letting me pick a name?" Beckett asks, shocked.

"No, we already picked names. We wanted to introduce you to Ellie Liesel Black. Her first name is inspired by this guy we know who sometimes goes by Eli."

Beckett's eyes fill with tears. "Ellie, it's beautiful."

"And this is Finn Beckett Black."

"Dammit guys, I'm so tired of crying," Beckett says as he breaks out into a full sob.

I hand him Finn to hold, and he rocks him gently in his arm. Even though he no longer has his right arm, he has no trouble holding them, changing their diapers, or anything else the babies need. He's a natural at being an uncle. After

Beckett has had his fill of Finn, he swaps him for Ellie, who loves being held by her uncle the most.

She coos softly as he holds her.

"Thank you, guys. I don't know what I did to deserve a part of both of their names, but thank you. I'm touched," Beckett says.

Both of the babies start crying, and I know what that sound means. They are hungry.

"Mealtime," I say.

Beckett gives me back Ellie and then leaves. Enzo helps me get settled into breastfeeding, and then he stands. "I'm going to go talk to Beckett for a minute. Do you need anything?"

"Nope, I'm perfect."

He kisses me on the forehead and then leaves to talk to Beckett.

An unsettling feeling washes over me because I know what they are discussing—what to do about Felix. What to do about the games Enzo and I have yet to finish. What to do about the men who want us dead.

Enzo promised to protect me and the babies. He promised he would do everything to save us. And the plan was to run until after the babies were born. Then fight.

It sounded like a good idea at the time. But now that the babies are here, I can't imagine Enzo and Beckett leaving me to go fight.

These babies need both of their parents. They need their uncle, their friends. They need them all.

I can't lose any of them. Not Enzo, Beckett, Liesel, or Langston. I'm done losing people. I want us all to move up to Alaska or any other town they choose. I want us to buy every house on the street and live happily ever after.

But listening to Enzo and Beckett's hushed voices down the hallway, talking battle strategy, I remember I don't always get my wish. The battle has to be fought, and the men are going to want me to sit this one out, for the babies' sakes.

I agree. I don't want to risk the babies' lives. I would never do that. But it's going to kill me to watch Enzo leave, and to wait, not knowing if he's going to live or die. Whatever we face, though, it's coming soon. Sooner than any of us want.

Felix thinks he's stronger, smarter than the rest of us. But he's never given birth. Never given everything you have for your children. He has no idea how strong and ruthless I have become. No idea the lengths I will go to protect my children. Felix will regret the day he decided to mess with me or my family.

23

ENZO

We got one month with the twins. One month to revel in our new role as parents. One month of peace. One month of happiness.

And then one text message changed everything.

"He found us," Beckett says, racing into our bedroom.

Kai is feeding Finn, and I'm rocking Ellie to sleep in my arms. He didn't knock. He didn't wait to make sure we were decent. He just barged in, and from the frantic look on his face, I know this is the moment our time is up.

I wanted to be the one to attack. Be on the offensive. But every time I formed a plan with Beckett, I couldn't go through with it. I couldn't leave these babies without provocation. I couldn't leave Kai. But it seems now is the time.

Beckett crawls up our bed and lays down between Kai and me, holding out his phone so we can all read the text message.

Felix has found us.

Or at least, he found Beckett's cell phone number.

. . .

FELIX: The final game is happening in one week. I'm giving you one week to prepare as a courtesy. I'm not a monster, after all.

I GRAB the phone from Beckett's hand and type furiously.

ME: You are a monster. We won't be coming. You can take the crown. We don't want it.

FELIX: I tried. I can't. Not without the final game. The men won't accept me as their leader. I can't get access to the money or weapons without the final game.

ME: We aren't coming.

FELIX: That's too bad. I don't usually like to kill children and pretty blondes but I will if you don't show up.

MY MOUTH GOES dry in panic. And then Felix sends pictures, and I about lose my shit.

The first one is of Liesel, tied to a chair in a dark room. Mascara is running down her cheeks, and a gag is in her mouth. She was the first girl I ever loved, not in the same way I love Kai, but she opened my heart to the ability to love Kai. And now...now Felix will kill her if I don't do something.

The second picture fills me with a rage I didn't know was possible until I became a father.

It's a picture of a young boy, around three years old, I would guess. His eyes are big and puffy from crying, he's in a small dark closet, and the bastard had the audacity to tie his little wrists together.

The child is my brother, well my half-brother, as every man and boy in my life turns out is related to me in some way. And that cuts me even worse, I not only didn't know of the boy's existence but failed in protecting him from a monster.

ME: Return the boy to his parents. Liesel is enough to get us to come.

FELIX: Oh, but, Liesel is his parent. And I think I'll be keeping him. Better motivation. One week. Meet in Miami where your house once stood. Both of you. If Kai doesn't show up, I'll kill the boy.

I CHUCK my phone hard against the wall as tears stream down my face. My little brother. Liesel, my sister, for all purposes, both taken by a madman because of me. I should have protected them, like I protected my own children. Instead, I was selfish. I put my own happiness above every-thing else. I could have attacked Felix any time during the last couple of weeks. I could have stopped this before he resorted to taking Liesel and her son.

Now, I failed. Again.

I stand and pace, my anger flowing through my veins,

pumping me with so much hate and frustration. *How could I have failed?*

"Enzo," Kai says cautiously, as she puts both babies in Beckett's arm. He's sitting in the bed watching us. She stands, and our eyes meet.

While my eyes are filled with pain and hate, her's are filled with love and compassion. I don't understand how she could feel that way at a time like this.

"This isn't your fault," she says.

"Yes, it is. I failed."

"No, you didn't. You haven't had a chance to fail. You didn't know Felix would take them. And you were doing everything you could to protect your family. To be there for your kids. You were keeping your vow to me and putting us first."

She strokes my cheek. "Now, we can fix this."

I grab her hand. "I can't lose you. Any of you. But—"

"I know. You won't. We have a week to figure out a plan. But we are not losing Liesel or that boy."

I close my eyes as tears replace my anger. Finn's cry stirs me deep in my soul. I have to do this for them. I have to do this for the boy Felix has trapped in a cage. I have to do this for Liesel, Langston, Beckett, Zeke. I have to do this for my mother. For Kai's birth parents. For her father.

I never wanted this, any of this. But this is what life gave me. A chance to change the Black organization forever. A chance to stop the evil that has been going on for generations.

I look from my children, to Beckett, to Kai. I couldn't pick a better army to help me.

"Let's destroy the evil once and for all," I say.

Kai smiles.

Beckett nods sternly, gripping the babies closely to his chest, like his arm alone is enough to protect them.

"One week," I grin. "That was Felix's mistake. Giving us a week to get ready."

We all nod.

"What are we going to do with the babies? Before I can discuss any attack plans, or how to destroy Felix and his army, I need to know our children are going to be safe, no matter what. I need to know if something happens to us, the babies are going to be taken care of and loved," Kai says.

"I can't—"

"No, we have to have a plan in case we both die fighting for them. They have to be safe," Kai says, not letting me think otherwise. We do need a plan, as much as it hurts me to think of Kai dying. Of our children growing up without a parent.

We both look to Beckett. He already loves our children. He would make a great substitute parent to our babies if it comes to that.

He looks down at the two bundles sleeping on his chest. "You know I love your children and would give my life for them. And I would be happy to raise them if anything happened to both of you. But you are going to need my help. I can't stay back and watch them while you go running off. I'm not the safe choice anyway. Felix knows I'm alive. He knows I flipped sides. If he wins, he'll come search for me —for us."

Beckett is right; I want him with us when we take on Felix. We need all the allies we can get. And Beckett is only a good choice if Felix and his men are dead along with us. Only then would Beckett be the safe choice to raise our babies.

I look at Kai, and we both have the same idea at the same time—"Langston."

"But where is he? How do we get in contact with him? Does Felix know he's alive?" Kai asks.

"I have a general idea where he might have gone. And yes, I can find him if I want to." I turn to Beckett. "Does Felix know Langston is alive?"

Beckett thinks for a moment. "I don't think so. He knew Liesel was alive. He saw the security footage of her crawling away from the car after the explosion. But he had no reason to suspect Langston lived. But if he suspects...he's good at finding people."

"We will make him think the twins are with my father," Kai says.

We all turn and face her. "He might have had footage of your father's death," I say.

"It's impossible to know for sure. There was so much smoke and debris. There would be no way for him to know for sure. We will tell him the twins are with my father. That way if we all die, and Felix is still alive; he'll be searching for a dead man, not Langston," Kai says.

We have a plan that at least ensures the twins will be safe. Now we just need to find Langston and get him somewhere safe with the twins. Then we can figure out how to kill Felix, without losing any more people we love.

24

KAI

"ARE YOU SURE YOU CONTACTED HIM?" I ask Enzo for the millionth time in the last three days. Time is running out for us to leave to go to Miami. And Langston still hasn't responded to Enzo's email.

"Yes, I'm sure," Enzo answers.

I pace the small two-bedroom cottage we bought with cash in New Zealand. We've been arguing for days about the best place to hide our babies with Langston. Ultimately, no place was safe enough. So we settled on a small town in New Zealand. It has no connections to us or Felix. It feels like a million miles away from Miami, and Enzo is pretty sure Langston is in Australia, so it will be easy for him to travel here.

We decided on a simple cottage to purchase. Although, we only put a modest down payment down, and we know that Langston has enough money to continue to make monthly payments on it. We decided against purchasing a large house outright or even paying off this mortgage. One of Felix's first moves would be to track down any large home purchases in the last week, assuming we would buy a house for whoever is watching our kids. So we decided against buying any house for them. Anything to make it harder for Felix to find them.

But we've been here for two days now, and Langston still hasn't shown up. I pace the room as I pump breast milk, and the babies sleep in a crib side by side. They each have their own crib, but it seems they sleep better when they are in the same crib. Side by side. Close together.

My nipples are sore and cracked from me pumping basically non-stop these last three days. I'm hoping to have enough breastmilk for my babies while I'm gone a couple of days. But if I don't make it, Langston will have to change to formula. Just one of the many ways my babies' lives will be different with me gone.

There is a light rapping at the front door. And we all freeze.

Is it him?

We all walk to the front door. Enzo looks through the small peephole, while Beckett grips his gun at his waist, and I stand behind them both hoping and praying it's Langston.

Enzo lets out a deep breath and opens the door.

Langston.

"Thank god," I say, running past Beckett and pushing Enzo out of the way as I take Langston into my arms.

He puts his arms around me carefully. "You're alive? How?"

I cry against his chest, the breast pump still doing its thing against my chest.

Langston grabs my shoulders and pulls me from his chest so he can look at me. His tears say more than words ever could.

"How are you alive?" and then he spots the breast pump. "You had the baby?" His eyes light up.

"Babies, actually," I say with a broad grin.

Enzo grabs Langston and I. "Get inside, you two, and stop making a scene for the neighbors."

We both step inside, and Enzo shuts the door behind us.

"I saw you die in the explosion. I was on the beach near your car. I watched you and Liesel die. How are you alive?" Langston asks.

"That would be me. I pulled her out of the car before the explosion," Beckett says.

Langston looks from me to Beckett.

"I'm Enzo's brother," Beckett says.

Langston's eyes go big. "You're Enzo's brother? How many brothers do you have, Enzo?"

Enzo frowns. "Four half-brothers. One biological brother. Two friends who I count as brothers. Probably more I'm not aware of. So a lot," he tries to laugh it off, but it is ridiculous how many men in his life are related to him.

Langston studies Beckett.

"He's one of the good guys, trust me," I say.

Langston smiles gently at Beckett. "If she trusts you, that's good enough for me."

"Would you like to meet the babies?" I ask, hoping he says yes, since the reason we brought him here is to take care of them and be their guardian if the three of us were to perish.

"Yes," he says, his face lighting up. But I can see what Enzo warned me about. Langston's eyes are tired, like he hasn't slept in months. His hair is longer than I've ever seen it. His usually clean-shaven face is scruffy. And although he has a nice tan from being out in the sun, he doesn't look healthy. He looks worn down and exhausted. I've never seen him like this.

But it doesn't make me doubt he's the right man for the job. If anything, the babies will help him heal faster.

We all walk into the small nursery I set up for the babies. It contains two cribs, a dresser, and a rocking chair.

I pick up our son and hand him to Langston. He takes him a little awkwardly in his arms at first, not sure exactly how to cradle his head, but after a moment he seems more at ease.

"This is Finn Beckett Black," I say.

He smiles at him and then registers the name. He looks at Enzo. "Finn? Really?"

Enzo nods proudly. "I named him after you and Zeke."

Langston tries to blink back his tears, but one escapes and slips down his cheek, landing on Finn's chubby cheek.

"Finn Black, nice to meet you," Langston says, now rocking him a little, seeming more natural as he holds my son.

"Would you like to meet our daughter?" I ask.

Langston nods.

I pick up Ellie, and Enzo takes Finn from Langston. I hand Ellie to Langston.

"Meet Ellie Liesel Black."

Langston closes his eyes in pain as I say her name, and I realize my mistake. Langston still thinks Liesel is dead. He doesn't know the truth. That Felix has her and is using her as ransom to get me and Enzo to finish the game.

"It's the perfect name," Langston says, staring down at her, already in love with our daughter as much as we are.

After rocking her a minute in his arms, he looks up. "Is Liesel..." he can't ask if Liesel is dead.

I open my mouth to speak, but Enzo jumps in.

"I'm sorry," is all he offers.

Langston nods, turning his attention back to Ellie.

I frown as I look at Enzo. *Why didn't you tell him Liesel is alive?*

Enzo looks me in the eyes. I understand his intentions. Langston needs to stay and take care of the babies. He's not fit enough to try and rescue Liesel. He would get himself killed. And if we aren't successful in saving Liesel, he won't survive learning she died all over again. This is for the best.

I bite my lip, not sure if my husband is right or not. Langston deserves to know Liesel is alive. But I trust him to know how Langston feels right now more than I do. And besides, if things work out, we will be bringing Liesel home with us.

"So we have something to ask you," I say to Langston.

Langston takes a deep breath looking from Ellie to Finn, then up to me. "I will protect these babies with my life."

25

ENZO

Beckett drives up in front of the beach that once was the site of my house, and is now the site of my pain.

This is where I thought I lost Langston and Liesel. This is the site where I thought I lost all my men. This is the site where I lost Kai and the babies.

I grip Kai's hand tighter; this is the site where I get it all back. This is where I protect everyone I love. This is where I get my revenge.

Beckett puts the car in park, and we all sit for a moment in silence, knowing once we step out of the car, there is no going back. We will fight Felix to the death. That is the only way to keep our family safe. Even if it means our deaths.

I look from Beckett to Kai. "Let's do this."

We all step out of the car ready for whatever tricks Felix has planned. And as we walk up the hill to where the remains of my house sit, I know we are in for a big fight.

Over a hundred men stand in the basement of my house, now exposed to the sun. Most are standing in a semi-circle around Felix. Others are off to the side, not really making it clear if they are behind Felix or not. All of them are men and women who used to work for me. Now, I don't know whose side they are on.

I resist the urge to draw my gun. I want to kill Felix immediately, but that would most likely be a death sentence. No matter how strong we are, the three of us can't take on a hundred men by ourselves.

"So happy you could join us," Felix says as we take a step onto the cement ruins. I loved this house, and Felix destroyed it.

I grin though, knowing I destroyed his home too.

Felix looks at Kai, "Already had the baby, I see? Too bad, I was hoping to be at the birth."

I step forward, needing to be between Kai and Felix, even though I know Kai is fully capable of taking care of herself.

"Have you run the DNA test yet? Have you determined which of my brothers is the father?" Felix asks, with a smug grin, thinking his words can hurt us. *They can't.*

"I already know who the father is," Kai says, gripping my hand. We have no doubt those babies are mine. They've always been mine. A DNA test won't prove anything other than what we already know.

Felix looks at me with a light in his eye. "Too bad, Milo was the better brother. Any child of his would have been amazing."

"Where is Liesel? The child?" I ask, tired of Felix's games, and we only just got here.

Felix whistles and a car door opens. Liesel is sitting in the back of an SUV, still tied up. She looks exhausted but not hurt. Felix didn't physically touch her, *thank fuck.*

He nods, and the door slams shut.

"And the child?" Kai asks.

Felix grins. "This isn't any place for a child."

She moves to attack him, but I grab her arm and hold her back. I don't like that we don't know where the child is either. But once we kill Felix, we will have all the time in the world to find him. Although, I suspect the child is here somewhere. Felix would want to be able to use him as leverage if things don't go his way.

"Now, for the reason we are all here. The game," Felix says, looking to his left.

One of the men pushes a scrawny man forward—Archard. He stumbles forward, holding onto his glasses and a piece of paper. He looks like he's been tortured and beaten. He's lost a lot of weight. And I realize now Felix has tried to get him to pass on the Black power to him. I don't know exactly what that entails, but I'm guessing the passwords to the vaults and bank accounts. I've never needed the access to run the company, as my father left plenty of his personal money to me to run the company with. But it appears no matter how badly Archard is tortured; he won't give up that information to Felix.

Maybe I was wrong about Archard after all. Maybe he is on our side.

"Read the rules of the final game," Felix yells to Archard.

Archard tries to stand tall and proud, but he can't. His body is too broken and hurt.

"The final game is simple. The participants will battle in twenty-minute increments to the death. Each round will involve deadly and deadlier weapons until a victor has been crowned," Archard reads.

Felix grins. "Can the rules be amended to include more participants?"

Archard frowns and reads the fine print of the contract.

"Only with a unanimous vote from the crew present at the final game."

Felix's eyes light up—he's going to join the game. He finally found a way. Most of the men here think he's a better leader. They will vote for him to enter. And even those who think Kai or I would make a better leader, will vote to allow Felix to enter. They won't cross Felix. And they will want me to kill Felix. This will ensure that that happens.

"All those in favor of allowing other participants who are blood-related to the Black or Miller line to enter the final game, raise your hand," Felix says.

One by one, each hand goes up as I knew they would.

"Unanimous," Felix says with a grin.

Archard sighs, but nods.

"To enter, you must prove you are blood-related and be able to name a blood relation as your heir. Other than Enzo and Kai, are there any other blood relatives who would like to throw their name into the battle to become the leader of the Black organization?" Archard asks.

"I would like to compete for the Black organization. I think the organization has been under terrible leadership. So many lives have been lost. Buildings destroyed because of poor leadership. I have what it takes to be your leader," Felix says, stepping forward.

Archard nods, expecting that. He opens his mouth to speak, but Beckett interrupts him.

"I too would like to throw my name in," Beckett says.

I grab his arm. "What are you doing? You can't enter. This is a battle to the death."

"I know. I don't leave my family out to dry. You will need me to help take down Felix," he says so only I can hear.

My heart breaks, but he's right. We need his help.

"And who are you?" Felix asks like he has no clue who he is.

"I'm your half-brother. Eli Beckett. You can call me Beckett."

Archard doesn't seem surprised and doesn't question the development. He knew of Beckett's existence.

I frown. *How many people knew of all my brothers that existed and never told me?*

"Fine. I will need each of you to name an heir, add a game to the future games, and then sign the contract. Let's start with Enzo."

I walk to Archard and take the piece of paper from his hand. "My heir is Finn Black, my son," I say. I hate naming him as my heir. I don't want him to have anything to do with this organization. I don't want him to compete in any games. But after today, I plan on destroying this organization once and for all. So it doesn't matter.

I write his name down, hating myself the entire time I do. Then I write rules to a stupid game that will never be played. And finally, I sign my name—Enzo Black. They can never take my name from me, even if my legal name is Rinaldi, Black is my last name. I will not let what the name has become change anything.

Archard studies the paper carefully. "Good." Then he looks to Kai. "Kai Miller."

She steps forward. "Kai Black, actually." She holds up her hand, displaying her wedding ring proudly.

Everyone gasps.

She grabs the piece of paper. "I name Ellie Black, my daughter, as my heir."

More gasps.

Felix grins. "Twins? How cute. Who is watching the little ones right now while mommy and daddy play?"

"My father," Kai says sternly, planting the seed we hope will be one small step of protecting our children if we die, giving Langston just a second of a head start in fleeing from Felix if we fail.

She writes her game furiously on the paper, then signs it, and hands it back to Archard.

He looks it over, then calls Felix.

He takes the paper. "I name my daughter, Ansley Black, as my heir."

I raise an eyebrow, not sure if he's lying or telling the truth about having a daughter. But I don't question him now. I want him to play. I want him to lose. Killing him during the game is the only way to ensure his followers don't kill us.

He scribbles his game on the piece of paper, then signs it and hands it to Archard.

"Eli Beckett," Archard says.

Beckett steps forward and takes the piece of paper. I realize now he doesn't have an heir to name. He frowns, looking at me like he's about to hurt me. "I name Liesel's child as my heir."

It hurts. But I know it was necessary. He needs an heir to participate.

He scribbles on the paper while holding it against his knee, then hands it back to Archard.

Archard nods.

"Two will compete at a time. Each round will involve more and more dangerous weapons until only one man or woman is left standing. That person will be the winner. That person will be given all the access codes that only I know. That person will be the leader of the Black organization."

Archard takes a blank piece of paper and rips it into

four. He writes one of our names on each of the pieces of paper. "Before each round, I will draw names to decide who is competing. The first round involves no weapons. You will be required to stay within a twenty-foot circle while competing. And can only use what is within the boundaries. If you are all still alive, we will continue to the next round where you will be given your first weapon." Archard rips a hat off a man standing near him and tosses the four pieces of paper into it.

He draws the first name. "Enzo will be competing against...,"

We all suck in a breath as we wait. *Please say, Felix.* I want to kill him the first round and get this over with.

"...Kai."

At least Kai is safe. I won't hurt her.

"Which means Beckett and Felix will be competing. Each round will last twenty minutes. Kai and Enzo you are up first."

Kai and I step forward into the circle while everyone else takes a step back. We remove our guns and knives, setting them outside the circle.

Archard sets his watch. "And go."

Neither Kai or I move, we just stand, staring at each other, refusing to fight.

"Pussies! You see, men, they won't even fight each other! They are weak! Undeserving of the title," Felix shouts.

We both ignore Felix.

"I love you, stingray."

"I love you, Black."

I take her hand, gripping it hard as I try to push out all the hate and gather all the love and strength to surround us. These could be my last few moments with Kai, and I'm going to savor every second.

Beckett laughs. "If you think love is a weakness, then you can't see straight. Look at them. Look how strong they are. I've never seen such strength. They are willing to do anything to protect those that they love."

"I told you Beckett was on our side," Kai whispers to me.

"I know, you are always right," I wink.

And then I kiss her. In front of everyone. I kiss her like this is my first and last time. My tongue pushes deep into her mouth, tasting everything. This kiss is greater than love. This kiss binds us together—ensuring that as long as one of us is alive, so is the other. Nothing can separate us.

Slowly, we stop, long after the twenty-minute timer went off.

We walk out of the circle hand in hand, with no snark remarks from Felix. The rest of the crowd silent, as if in awe of what they just witnessed.

We walk over to Beckett. "Are you ready for this?" Kai asks.

Beckett nods.

"He can't use a weapon. Your job is just to run and tire him out. Get him frustrated. You aren't going to be able to kill him this round. The more he swings and misses, the more exhausted he's going to feel. Twenty-minutes is a long time to fight without a weapon. I'll distract him if I can with snide remarks," I say.

"I got this."

I hold my hand out, and we bump fists. "I know you do, brother."

He smiles and then steps into the ring with Felix. Both men remove their weapons, setting them outside the ring. Then face each other head to head.

I have no doubt that before Beckett lost his arm, this would've been a fair fight, but now I'm nervous. Beckett has a lot of rage built up about losing his arm because of this bastard. He has a lot of incentive to live and protect his niece and nephew. But I'm not sure if the will to live is stronger than skill and strength.

"Go," Archard says.

The two men take their time, circling each other, and feeling each other out.

"Nice to meet you, brother," Felix says. "Too bad it's going to be a short meeting." And then Felix swings, hard and fast.

He connects with Beckett's jaw, and Kai screams as blood shoots from his mouth. I grab Kai and pull her to my chest, covering her face with my hand so she can't see. Beckett doesn't need her distracting him.

But when I see Beckett's face, there is a grin there. I take a deep breath; he's got this. He let him hit him. He won't again.

Sure enough, that is Beckett's plan. To let Felix know what it's like to hit him. How good it feels, and then never give him the chance again.

For the next fifteen minutes, Beckett dances around the circle, never throwing a single punch, but letting Felix throw many. He misses every time, because Beckett is focused on avoiding and tiring Felix out, instead of connecting with him.

Felix is exhausted and angry.

And that makes me happy, but also scares me, because it only takes one wrong move for Felix to do damage.

"Not willing to fight, you pussy. I guess I wouldn't want to fight either if I only had one arm," Felix tries to goad Beckett.

It won't work.

Four more minutes they fight, until there is only one minute left. But one minute is all Felix needs to do damage.

Beckett makes one wrong step in his exhaustion. And Felix takes advantage. He connects with Beckett's jaw while grabbing his arm, making Beckett practically defenseless. Beckett tries to kick, to get Felix away, but Felix holds tight to his arm as he pounds into Beckett's face, breaking his nose, a tooth, and doing serious damage to his eye socket.

Kai tries to look, but I hold her tight against my chest, knowing the sight will be too much for her.

Come on, time.

I look at Archard who is frantically counting down the seconds.

"Ten seconds left," he shouts, almost egging Beckett on. He doesn't want Felix to win either.

Ten.

Nine.

Eight...

I count down the seconds as Felix gets more punches in.

"You got this, Beckett!" I shout, needing him to hang on and stay alive for just a few more seconds.

One more vicious punch before Archard yells time. Felix drops Beckett to the floor, and then Kai and I are running to his side.

I pull Beckett up and drape his arm around me. "Good job," I say.

He laughs. "I think I lost. You shouldn't be telling me good job."

"He fought dirty, and you know it. But you did what you needed to," I say as I walk Beckett to our side.

We all look over at Felix who is breathing heavily and barking at one of his men to help him bandage up his bleeding knuckles.

"He's going to struggle to use his hand in the next round. This is a team effort," I say.

Beckett nods.

"Alright, everyone survived round one. Which means on to round two. This game will involve one small knife." Archard produces two ridiculously small knives.

I sigh, these games are going to last forever. Just give us a gun and get this over with.

He puts all of our names back into the hat. Kai is kneeling on the floor, trying her best to dress Beckett's wounds when Archard calls out my name again.

"Enzo will be fighting in round two against..."

He draws a second name. "Beckett."

"No," Beckett and I say at the same time. We both stare at Kai who is just realizing what this means, and then we all look at Felix.

If Beckett and I are fighting each other, it means that Felix will fight Kai. She stands up, giving her fiercest stare to Felix. If the weapon was a gun, I would say it is a fair fight. Kai is unstoppable with a gun in her hand. She could kill Felix before he even got a chance.

But with a tiny knife, all it takes for him to win is to catch her. Physically he's stronger. He could choke her. Slam her head into the ground. Or use the knife to spill her blood from any major artery. Her only chance is to do what Beckett did and avoid him. But that didn't turn out so well for Beckett. Now Felix is angry, and I don't think he will settle this time for just spilling some blood. He's looking to kill.

And I don't know how to stop it from happening.

26

KAI

Enzo and Beckett look at me with concern as the names are read. But I'm not worried. They think because I just gave birth to two twins a few weeks ago that I'm weak. They think because I'm less than half the size of Felix that he's stronger. That because his muscles are bigger he's going to win. That there is no way I will leave this fight without being seriously damaged or dead.

They are wrong.

If I learned one thing giving birth to my twins, it's that I am strong.

That becoming a mother changed me in a way I didn't realize was possible. I thought I knew what love was, but not until I gave birth did I truly understand. Not until I heard those precious cries. Not until I felt them suckling at my breast. Not until I kissed their sweet lips did I understand love.

Love is strength.

Love is fierce.

Love is everything.

I may not seriously wound Felix. I may come out

looking as bad as Beckett. But I will win this battle. I will not be defeated. Because I am stronger than any of the men realize.

Archard calls for Enzo and Beckett to enter the ring that has been expanded to the edge of the property that hangs over a cliff—adding another layer of danger as falling over the edge would mean death. They take the knives from him, and he yells go.

But instead of fighting, they sit in the middle. Enzo tries to help Beckett take inventory of his wounds. And I try to read their lips as they discuss a strategy to keep me safe while defeating Felix. I know they won't let me die. I know if it looks like Felix is going to kill me when it's my turn, they will sacrifice themselves to ensure I win.

Finally, Archard yells, "Stop."

The two men walk out, giving me a look that confirms they have a plan to intervene. That I have nothing to worry about. But I don't want them to intervene. I want to do some damage to Felix. I've earned that right.

I walk over to Archard and retrieve my weapon—a small knife. I think back to the last time I had a knife driven into my skin. That pain was nothing.

Felix grins as he steps into the expanded ring with me. I see the edge of the cliff. I hear the waves crashing up against it. That would be my best shot at killing Felix. Not with this flimsy knife, but by pushing him over the edge.

"I'm going to enjoy this," Felix says.

I grip the knife tighter. "Me too."

I shoot once last glance at Enzo, who tells me with his eyes to be careful. Just stay safe. Do what Beckett did. And get Felix to give up his knife.

I nod, but I don't plan on playing it safe.

We are bringing Felix down together. And I plan on doing my part the same as Beckett and Enzo.

"Go," Archard says.

We both grip our knives. My first task is to get Felix to release his.

So I do the same thing Beckett did. I dance around the ring, giving Felix no chance to get close to me.

"So that's how this is going to go? You're going to run from me like you always do?" Felix says.

My eyes darken, and I dig my feet into the ground, stopping for just a second before I spring again. "Don't think you can hit me from across the circle."

He growls and throws the knife at me like I knew he would. The knife grazes my shoulder before flying past me out of the circle.

"You missed," I grin.

"I wasn't aiming for you."

I turn and see the knife sticking into Beckett's shoulder. He growls and removes the knife, throwing it to the floor.

"Didn't you ever learn not to poke momma bear?" I ask.

He cocks his head to the side. "You look more like a momma deer. Barely capable of saving herself, let alone protecting her young."

I smirk. "You're wrong."

I throw my knife hard and fast, hitting Felix hard in the gut, knowing it will knock the wind out of him, even though it won't do any serious damage. It does what I need it to do.

He gasps for air as he grips the knife lodged in his stomach. And I charge.

I hear Enzo and Beckett scream from behind me, but I can't hear them. All I know is I have to protect my children. And that means protecting their father and uncle too.

I run with everything I have. All of my anger. All of my rage, my fear, my protectiveness. It all comes with me.

I drive everything I have into knocking Felix over the edge.

I succeed.

The force is enough to push him over the edge.

But unfortunately, I can't stop myself from falling right along with him.

We both go over the cliff, but the force isn't enough to knock us away from the edge.

Felix grabs hold of the cliffside, while I grab hold of his leg.

Fuck.

My life is now tied to Felix's. I can't kill him without killing myself. And I can't die. My babies need me.

So all I can do is hold onto his leg as I dangle thirty-plus feet in the air and hope Felix can hang on.

"Kai!" I hear Enzo shout.

I look up and see Enzo, Beckett, and Archard standing over them.

"Hold on! We are lowering a rope," Enzo shouts.

But then Archard interrupts. "You can't help them, not for another ten minutes. If you do, you are automatically disqualified. And the penalty for helping them is death."

Felix looks down at me. "Hear that, momma deer? Who are you going to choose? Yourself or Enzo? Do your precious babies get to grow up with their mother or their father?"

"Both," I say, holding on tighter to Felix as I try my best to dig my feet into the cliffside, so I'm not relying on Felix so much. But my feet barely reach.

Felix chuckles. He tries to swing his leg to knock me

loose, but every time he does, he almost loses his balance himself.

So instead, we just dangle on the cliffside for ten minutes, waiting for the seconds to tick by—neither of us moving. Knowing one move could kill our enemy but take ourselves down along with them.

Finally, Archard yells, "Time's up!"

Two ropes are lowered. I grab one, while Felix grabs the other, and we are pulled up. When I reach the top, Enzo and Beckett both tackle me in a bear hug.

"Ten minutes has never gone by so slowly," Enzo weeps.

I pant heavily, my heart racing as I realize how close I came to death. If Felix had wanted to kill me, all he had to do was let go.

I stare over at Felix who is on all fours panting hard, just as exhausted as I am.

"Felix is tired. Now is the time to finish him off," I say.

Enzo and Beckett both stare at me. And Enzo grabs my face, "Never do that again. You scared us both to death."

"We can only take him down together. Now if they draw your name, you will be able to finish him easily," I say.

Enzo kisses my forehead. "I love you, stingray."

"I love you too, Black."

Archard steps into the center again. "The third round you get a gun with a single bullet."

Finally. A round Enzo and I can win. Especially with Felix so exhausted.

Archard puts all our names in and begins the drawing process again.

"Enzo will fight this round against..."

"...Kai."

Dammit.

We both look at Beckett. He's the weakest shot out of the

three of us. And he's the most beat up. I'm not sure he can win this round. And I can't watch him die.

"I know, it's okay. I got this," Enzo whispers into my hair.

I don't know what's going on in his head, but I trust Enzo. I know he has a plan to end this. I trust him.

I just nod.

Enzo stands and holds out his hand to me. I take it as he pulls me up. Archard has two guns loaded with one bullet a piece, and then he hands them to us.

"Good luck," Archard says.

I frown, feeling closer to the end of the game as I've ever felt before. But I don't know why this feels like the end. Enzo and I aren't going to fight. It's Beckett we have to worry about. This round will be another twenty minutes of time-wasting. Hopefully, Enzo will tell me the plan this time.

We step into the circle together, armed with our guns.

Archard yells, "Go."

And then Enzo pulls me into a hug against his chest. He buries his mouth in my hair so no one can see his lips move or hear what he is going to say to me.

"I got a glance of the paper with each round on it," Enzo says.

I don't react, although this surprises me. I guess Archard is on our side after all.

"It continues just like this round for three more rounds. For three more rounds, you only get a gun with a single bullet in it."

I nod. "That's good. We are better shots than Felix. Beckett just has to dodge the bullet this next round. Then you or I can kill Felix."

Enzo kisses my head. "Don't shoot first. Let Felix get his shot. Then fire."

I nod, agreeing, but I don't know why we are talking

about what I should do against Felix, when we don't even know who will face Felix. Beckett could still win. We need to be thinking about how to get him to win.

"I love you, stingray."

"I love—"

But his lips crash down on mine. And I'm lost to the kiss. I'm floating high above all the danger, above all the pain. Love conquers all—I know that when I kiss Enzo. There is no way Felix will win.

But then the kiss stops, broken abruptly.

My eyes are closed, but I feel the loss sweep through me. It's more than the loss of a kiss. It's the loss of love.

I open them, and I realize Enzo's plan. To ensure I'm the one who wins. I'm the one who lives.

I watch as he runs for the cliff.

"No!" I shout as I run after him. There has to be another way. But I know Enzo has made up his mind. He thinks the only way to keep me alive is if I win the game. But after we beat Felix, surely we can convince the men we can rule together. But the angry eyes looking at me from all directions tells me that is a false hope. They will make us stay and fight until only one of us lives.

I run as hard and as fast as I can. For myself. For my babies. Enzo can't die. There has to be another way. But as fast as I can run, I know that it's not enough. Enzo is faster.

He flings himself off the edge of the cliff at the same time I dive for him. I grab his arm, and he dangles over the edge with me holding onto this arm with everything I have.

"You can't die," I plead, holding onto him as tears fall down my cheeks.

"I was never meant to live."

"No," I shake my head. "We are one. We live. I need you. Our babies need you."

He looks at me tenderly. "I know. And this is what I have to do. You know it. I know it. The world knows it. I deserve to pay for the sins I committed. This is the only way to save you. These men won't let us all walk out of here alive. Only one will leave. Only one will survive. That has to be you. Our babies need you. You are the only one strong enough to survive with everyone else dead. I've already proven I'm not strong enough. But you are. You were thriving without me. You are strong enough."

"No, I'm not," I cry, more tears falling. My arms are exhausted and tired from clinging to Felix earlier. I can't hold on much longer. And Enzo doesn't want me to.

"I love you. I can't live without you," I plead.

"I'll never leave you. We are one. I'll always be with you, even when I'm gone. Death will never part us."

I sob full on at his words. This can't be how our story ends. This can't be the end.

We are supposed to get our happily ever after. We are supposed to get to live. We are supposed to go back to the cottage in New Zealand. Or live in the mansion in Alaska. Or sail the seas on our yacht. Not this...

This can't be real.

But I know that it is.

"It's okay. Let go, Kai. I will always be with you. Death can't separate us."

Another tear falls, and I know it's the end. The tear lands on my hands, and I lose everything. My hands slip, and I watch Enzo fall.

Death shouldn't be peaceful, at least not dying young. But watching Enzo fall felt peaceful. Until he was gone. When the waves swept his body under them, and I could no longer see him. That's when the peace was taken.

I sob into my hands as I'm completely broken. I can't

think. I can't breathe. All I can do is cry.

I feel arms around me, but I don't know whose arms. I'm lost. Enzo was wrong. I can't survive this. I should have fallen over the cliff with him. I can't survive to be a mother for our babies, not without him.

"You are strong," Beckett says, pulling me back.

But I don't feel strong.

"Enzo loved you. I love you," he kisses me on the cheek before stepping into the ring.

I hear Archard yell, "Go." And I finally snap out of my heartbreak enough to realize what is about to happen.

Beckett drops his gun.

"No!" I scream. "Fight back!"

But Enzo and Beckett had a plan, to ensure that I lived. That I would be the victor. That if only one of us survived, it would be me.

Felix smirks, looking at me like I'm next. And then he shoots Beckett in the chest.

He falls instantly to the ground.

I scream, but it comes out of me in slow motion, just like Beckett's fall to the ground.

Archard snaps his fingers. And men run into the circle, grab Beckett's body, and drag him away.

Two men I love—dead.

Two men who loved me sacrificed everything for me.

Archard breaks the silence. "The remaining rounds are the same. You will each be given a gun with a single bullet and twenty minutes to fight. If neither of you is successful in killing the other after twenty minutes, we will reset and start again until one of you is the victor."

I stand from my broken spot on the ground and wipe the tears and snot on the back of my hand. I will not let their deaths be in vain. I will win. I will defeat Felix.

I walk into the circle calmly. Archard loads the two guns and hands one to Felix and one to me.

"It's going to feel so good when I win. The first thing I'm going to do is hunt down those babies of yours—Finn and Ellie. Beautiful names. Staying with your father, you said?"

I growl.

Felix laughs as he tosses his gun from hand to hand. "That was a lie, Kai."

I narrow my eyes.

"You thought you could fool me? Really? I've been one step ahead this entire time."

"Go!" Archard shouts.

I grip my gun and wait for Felix to shoot at me like Enzo warned. I need to dodge the bullet first, then shoot him. I can't be caught off guard. But apparently, Felix is in no hurry to kill me. He keeps talking.

"Actually, the first thing I'm going to do when I win is have my way with Liesel. She's a hot piece of ass, don't you think?"

Don't be goaded. Be ready for the shot.

Felix tosses the gun back to his left hand.

"I'll keep her around for a few weeks until she's broken. Then I'll kill her." He tosses the gun back to his right.

"Her child is of no use to me. I'll have one of my men kill him." He tosses it back to his left. He's not left-handed. He's a good shot with his right, but a terrible with his left.

"And then, I'm coming for your children."

I growl as he tosses the gun back to his right hand.

"But they aren't hiding with your father. They are hiding with Langston."

He tosses the gun to his left hand, and I take my shot.

I fire, aiming right for his heart.

He realizes his mistake a second too slow. He tries to fire

with his left hand, but misses any serious organ, and instead hits my shoulder. But I hit my target—his heart.

I watch him fall slowly to his knees as blood spills from his chest. I walk over to him so I can watch the life leave his eyes.

I stand over him as he falls back, but his chest still rises and falls for another second, for one more beat of his heart —spilling more blood.

"You lose. I win. Love wins. Beckett sacrificed his life to save me. Enzo sacrificed his life to save me and our kids. They both knew I was stronger than you. Because love is stronger than hate. Love is stronger than evil."

And then Felix stops breathing. He's gone—dead.

I'm safe. My children are safe. But the sacrifice that was made was great. The loss was everything.

I close my eyes as the tears fall. There is much to do. I have to figure out what to do with the men. I have to set Liesel and her child, free. I have to tell Langston the news. I have to find a way to tell my babies about what their father and uncle did to protect me.

But that can all wait. My heart is broken—a piece of it gone forever over the cliff and into the ocean. I tried to save him. But it wasn't enough. The only way to protect them all was to stay dead, to stay hidden, because only one of us could survive. Only one got to live.

But I failed at staying dead, and now Enzo is gone forever.

Death will never part us. Enzo's words ring in my ear.

Then why do I feel so alone? Why do I feel so cold? Because death won. We are apart. There is no happily ever after. Just survivors, trying to find a way to live without the love they lost.

27

KAI

I'VE BEEN LYING on the ground for over an hour. And I felt every second of it. I know the pain I felt. Time didn't move faster or slower. It just kept ticking, moving on like I didn't exist.

I can't keep laying here on the ground—suffering in my heartbreak.

I have to get up. I have to set things right. I have to go be a mother.

But standing up and opening my eyes to the pain is the hardest thing I've ever done.

I do it, but just barely. And when I open my eyes, I'm shocked by what I see.

There is a group of men tied up with guns pointed at their heads off to one side. All men who were Felix's loyal followers. But there is a larger group staring at me. And as I stand, they fall down to one knee.

My eyes shoot around and watch as every man and woman kneels in front of me.

"What's happening?" I ask, to no one in particular.

Clifton steps forward from the crowd. I hadn't even realized he was here. "They are accepting you as their new leader. Every man and woman bowing will go to the ends of the earth for you. They will fight for you. Protect your children with their lives. You won the games, and won them all over."

Wow.

I expected once I won, I would have the power. I didn't expect the men to actually honor that I was their leader. At least, not like this.

"The men would like to know what you would like to do with the betrayers?" Clifton asks.

I look at the men who would kill me or my children in a heartbeat. "Kill them, but not here. Enough blood has been spilled here."

Clifton nods and heads toward the men to be disposed of.

Archard steps forward. "You are now Kai Black, the leader of this organization. And with it comes all the powers and benefits, along with the responsibilities."

"I've always been Kai Black," I say solemnly. Winning the game changed nothing.

Archard nods, as do most of the men agreeing with me.

"I will now transfer the codes and locations of the vaults and bank accounts," Archard says.

I nod.

He leans down and whispers into my ear so only I can hear. I'm afraid at first I will forget, but this is what I've fought so hard for. There is no way I will forget.

"My job is done," Archard says once he has finished telling me the codes, and then he leaves after giving my hand a tight squeeze.

I look over to the man closest to me. "Release Liesel," I order.

The man stands and makes a call, and the van returns. A door opens, and Liesel steps out.

I run to her, needing the comfort of one of my only friends left in the world. We collide in an embrace full of pain at losing a man we both loved.

"I'm sorry, I failed," I say.

She grabs my face and looks at my tear-streaked eyes. "No, you won. Love won."

"Your child!" I look around for someone, anyone, to tell me where her son is. "Where is he?" I shout to the nearest man.

"I don't know, Black," he says.

"It's Mrs. Black," I say.

"Sorry, Mrs. Black. But I will find out for you right away."

I nod and turn back to Liesel.

"I can't see him," she says suddenly.

"Why not?"

"Because he needs to go back to his parents. I don't want him in this life. I don't want to have to choose someday between saving my child and the man I love. It's not safe for him. And if I see him, I won't be able to let him go," Liesel says.

If my heart could break again, it would for her.

"I understand," I say, instead, wrapping her in a hug again.

"Where will you go? Will you come with me? Langston is watching the babies. You two deserve a happily ever after even if I don't get one."

She's silent for a second. "I can't come with you. I just need to go. To disappear. I'm not cut out for this life."

I sigh, but nod. "Can I at least tell Langston you are alive in case he wants to try and find you?"

"No, I don't want him to find me. It's best he thinks I'm dead."

I disagree. The man is heartbroken; I don't care what she says. But that's a fight for another day. Eventually, I'll tell Langston the truth, but I'll let Liesel have her space first.

"Promise me you won't tell him?" she asks.

"I'll keep your secret for as long as I can," I say.

She nods. "Thank you."

"Do you need money? A car? A bodyguard?"

She smiles. "I'll take a car to the airport. But I have plenty of money." She hugs me one final time. And then I watch as she walks away to the car she was a captive in just a few minutes ago.

I stand until she disappears down the road, and then I walk to the edge of the cliff where Enzo's house once stood. I glance down over the edge and watch as the tide rolls higher and higher, hitting hard against the edge of the cliff. When we lived here, the water rarely came this high, but it does now.

I stare for a long time, hoping somehow the ocean saved him. Hoping somehow this isn't the end. But the ocean doesn't give Enzo back to me. It claimed him, and now he's gone.

"We found the child, Mrs. Black. Would you like to see him?" a man says.

"Yes, please."

I turn around and do my best to leave the pain behind, even though it's going to follow me forever.

I follow the man to another car. The door opens, and a young boy flings himself into my arms. I catch him, and my heart heals the tiniest of bits. This boy is safe because of Beckett and Enzo's sacrifice. Because we won.

I hold him tightly in my arms. I don't know how he senses that I'm here to save him. Maybe it's because I'm the first woman he's seen. Maybe it's because he just needs to believe it. But he grips my neck tighter as I lift him out of the car.

"Are you here to save me?" he asks.

"Yes, I'm here to save you. You're safe." I kiss his chubby cheek. And stare into the brown eyes of a boy that looks so much like Enzo it hurts. Enzo will live on, I realize. In this child, in Finn, in Ellie, in me. He will live on, and that has to be worth living for.

"What's your name?" I ask.

"Black," he says back.

I grin. "That's my name too."

"It's also my favorite color."

"It's a good color," I agree. I don't know if his first name is really Black. I don't know if his adoptive parents decided to keep it as his last name or middle name. It doesn't matter. He is family. And he's safe.

Liesel may be afraid, but that's normal for what she's been through. She will come around. And one day she might meet the son she gave up once she realizes the world is safe. I will never let the world be dangerous again for our kids' sakes.

"Can I drive you home, Mr. Black?" I ask.

He frowns, staring at the car he just jumped into my arms from.

"Can we walk?"

I laugh, not blaming the little one. "We can walk for a bit. Then how about I get you a convertible to ride in? Those don't have tops. They aren't scary; they are fun."

He nods, smiling brightly.

I look to the man watching us, and with one look he's headed to get a convertible here as fast as possible so I can drive the little boy home before I return to find my own babies.

28

KAI

Six Months Later

"I'm still not sure what I'm going to do about the Black organization. Do I destroy it? Sell it? Rule it?" I say to Langston.

"That's why you need to get away from it all for a while. Take the babies and just get away," Langston responds as he helps me pack the twins' clothes into a bag.

"Come with me," I say.

He frowns. "You know I love the twins, but I need a break. I need time to mourn my own losses. I need to figure out what I want."

I gnaw on my lip, trying to decide if now is the time to tell him or not. We've been living in Miami in a hotel room for the last six months. I've been running the Black organization from here, while Langston has helped with the twins. We've both been so busy we have barely had time to mourn.

But now that everything has settled, it's time. Time to

mourn. Time to make the tough decisions about our future. And I think it's time Langston knows the truth.

"What aren't you telling me?" he asks.

"I think you should sit," I say.

"No, I think I'll stand."

I sigh. "Langston, there is something I've kept hidden from you.

"At first, we didn't tell you because you weren't in a good place. And if something happened to her, we didn't think you could mourn her twice and survive. But then she survived, and she asked me not to tell you. She wanted space."

"Who?" he asks, but I can already see his heart breaking.

"Liesel—she's alive."

His knees weaken, and he falls, luckily a rocking chair is behind him to break the fall.

He sits in the chair, his eyes glazed over. "Liesel is alive?"

"Yes."

"And she didn't want me to know?"

"Yes."

I watch his face twist, his heart throb in pain. I think knowing Liesel wanted him to think she was dead might be worse than her actually being dead.

Suddenly, he stands up. "I need to go."

"Wait!" I chase after him as he walks out of the hotel room.

"Kai, I love you. I will find you in a few months once I've dealt with this pain and betrayal, but right now I just need time."

I stop at the door. "I understand. I'm sorry."

He walks back and gives me a hug. "You aren't the one who should be saying sorry."

"I love you."

"I love you, too."

And then he's gone. And I'm alone with the twins. I'm supposed to take some time to decide what is best for me and the twins, and there is only one place I can imagine going where I can think. One place in the world that was only ever Enzo and mine's. One place that all the people who knew of its existence are now dead—Alaska.

———

I WALK into the house my father bought for me in Alaska, carrying a child under each arm. I can say one thing—my arms have gotten a lot stronger over these last six months.

But the second we step inside, I know this is right. This is home. I don't know what this means for the Black organization. I don't know what this means for our future, but this is where my heart is.

"We are home," I say.

"Took you long enough."

I look up and see two angels.

I should know by now people can return from the dead. But not when I watched them die with my own eyes.

I set each crawling child down and run straight for Enzo. The twins start crawling hurriedly when they spot their father and uncle.

Enzo grabs me in his arms and spins me around as his lips crash down on mine before we collapse on the floor as the twins reach us. He scoops them both up in his arms while never letting go of me.

We are all crying and kissing and hugging. And then I remember Beckett. I hold my arms out, and he joins the kissing and hugging fest.

"You're both alive," I whisper.

They cry their responses.

"What took you so long to come here?" Beckett cries.

"I knew it would hurt the most coming here. Because this place reminded me the most of both of you."

Enzo kisses both of our children who are delighted but also trying to crawl away to explore. But he won't let them go.

"Jesus, they've gotten so big. I missed so much," Enzo says.

"But you won't miss anymore," I say.

Enzo and Beckett have fallen silent, and I realize I'm missing part of their plan.

"We are alive, but only because everyone thinks we are dead. When you go back to Miami, we have to stay hidden here. We can only have these brief moments of happily ever after," Enzo says.

I frown.

"No, I just got you back. I'm Mrs. Black now. I'm their leader. I have the money, the resources, the power. They will let you live if I tell them to," I say.

Beckett gives me a look, though, and I know I'm wrong.

"Was this your guys' plan all along? To fake your deaths?" I ask.

"Sort of..." Beckett says looking to Enzo for help.

"We were both willing to sacrifice ourselves for you. For these kids. We knew you had to live. We knew you could defeat Felix, which we are so fucking proud of you for. So that's what we did. We died. I'm just lucky the tide was high enough to break my fall, and I can hold my breath for a long time, and I'm an excellent swimmer. I swam away and only surfaced when I was far enough away I didn't think anyone could see me."

"Well, it worked. Because I've thought you were dead this entire time." I look from Enzo to Beckett.

"I just got lucky Felix is a bad shot. He missed my heart and lungs by millimeters. The men didn't check if I was breathing after I dropped, they just dragged me off. They left me alone in the back of the truck before they buried me. I fled. I guess they didn't tell you they lost my body," Beckett says.

I think back to the burial service I had for Beckett and Enzo. They both have markers on the ledge Enzo fell from. I just assumed Beckett's body had actually been buried there. They dug a hole and everything.

I look at both men and slap them hard across the cheek.

"Don't ever do that to me again! You don't get to sacrifice yourself. There is always another way," I say.

But then I grab both of their necks, hugging them as we all cry again, so happy it all worked out. They are alive. Even if I only get them in small bursts.

There is a small rapping on the door, and we all freeze. Beckett and Enzo draw their guns. And I wipe my tears, gripping my own gun in my jeans, before I walk to the door. I look through the peephole and see Clifton, one of my most loyal men.

I let go of my gun in my waistband and open the door.

"Yes, Clifton? What are you doing here? I told you I didn't want to be disturbed unless it was urgent," I say.

He moves out of the way, and I see fifty men standing in my driveway.

"This is urgent," he says.

I step onto my front porch, feeling tense. I don't know what the hell is happening. "What's going on?"

Silence.

"Clifton, what's happening?"

But one of the other men steps forward. "Is Enzo here? Is he alive?"

Panic shoots through me. We are outnumbered fifty to three. If they want him dead, they will kill him. And again, I would have to choose between my husband and my children. My kids are inside. I can't let them hurt them.

"Is that why you are all here? To try and kill a dead man? Go home! All of you! I've given my everything to running this empire for the last six months, and now when I want to rest and mourn in peace for a month, you all show up at my doorstep and bring up the love of my life— whose death I will never get over. Really? That's how you repay my loyalty to you? With distrust? You all just made my decision much easier. I thought I wanted to keep this company running. I thought we could find a way to do something good with what generations have built. But I was wrong." Tears stream, but I'm not sure if it's from fear or being hurt by men and women I thought were loyal to me.

I start walking back inside, hoping I said enough to get them to leave. But Enzo and Beckett will need to find a new place to hide out in.

"Mrs. Black, I'm sorry. We didn't mean to bring up the past or your pain. But we saw how hard you fought for Enzo. How much you loved each other. And many of us now realize we were wrong to make you choose. You have children who you love, but it's never stopped you from being a great leader. We were just hoping somehow against all odds Enzo survived. We want to see you happy. We think you fight better with him by your side. We just hoped our queen got her king."

I blink. I must have misheard. This can't be happening.

But then the door is opening, and Enzo steps out.

I don't know if he heard what the man said, or if he's just trying to prevent a fight from happening near our kids.

But when he steps out, then men start bowing down to Enzo as they did to me.

Enzo walks over to me and holds me around the waist. "Well, look at that. Some members of our team are loyal to us. Love wins, after all."

He kisses me tenderly on the lips.

A moment later, Beckett steps out, carrying the twins and the men and women light up seeing our entire family together.

Not every person who works for us is here. It might still be a fight. But we have a large loyal group who wants us to lead them. They believe our love makes us better leaders.

"If we are going to continue to lead this organization, there are going to be some changes made," I say.

"Yes!" everyone shouts as they stand back up.

"For one," I pull the stupid contract with all the children's names on it. "We will no longer play ridiculous games to decide who the next leader is. If Enzo and I were to both die, then the group will vote on who their next leader is."

"Yes!" everyone shouts.

I hold the contract up, and someone tosses Enzo a lighter. He lights it, then we all watch as the contract burns. My children are safe from ever having to compete. Liesel's child is safe. Even Felix's child, if she does exist, is safe.

Our family still has a hard future ahead. We will always have enemies. We will always have allies who turn against us. We will always have family that pops up in unexpected ways. But we will also always have each other.

I kiss Enzo on the lips as we start planning our new life together. One where we don't live in the shadows. One where we don't have to die in order to live.

"Truth or lie," I start.

Enzo smiles and then waits for me to finish.

"Truth or lie—now we live happily ever after?"

"Truth."

EPILOGUE

KAI

Five Months Later

"Hurry up! The twins' birthday party starts in three hours," Enzo says as I walk to the door.

I laugh. "I'll be back in an hour. The decorations are already finished. All you have to do is pick up the cake and get them dressed."

He kisses me on the lips. "Fine, go. Go be Mrs. Black. I'll wait here like the nobody I am."

I laugh. "You were the one who let me win. You could have fought harder," I say.

He waves me off, not wanting to get into the argument again. For the past few months, we have found our roles when it comes to running the empire. I found our purpose —protecting innocent lives by saving women from domestic violence and human trafficking, and feeding and helping children who were abused find good homes.

Enzo helps ensure the money keeps rolling in by selling

technology, yachts, and weapons to our allies, but only to those who aren't hurting innocent lives.

Beckett has found a knack for building new technologies and is key to the development of new security systems we sell.

We all have our roles to play. It makes us better, stronger.

Even though the men and women accept our leadership as a unit, I'm still the one in charge. If there is a disagreement about anything, I'm the one who gets final say.

It drives Enzo crazy. Even Beckett struggles with it sometimes when he disagrees with my decision. But it is what it is. If they didn't want me to lead, then they shouldn't have sacrificed their lives to make it so.

Today, we are celebrating the twins' birthday, but I got an urgent message from Archard saying he hasn't gotten word yet that I visited the vault and changed the entry codes. He said they expire today and everything inside will be lost forever if I don't go use the code.

I'm the only one who is allowed the codes and allowed to enter the vault, so I'm going alone.

The vault is where Surrender, the club, once stood. But the vault survived the explosion.

I drive my Maserati to the site and follow Archard's instructions to the stairs leading down to the vault still there, buried beneath the rubble. He had some of the men move enough of the rocks out of my way so I can find it.

I get to the door and enter the ridiculous string of letters and numbers I have no idea how I remember, but I do. And then I pause. I don't know what's behind this door. I'm sure riches and more wealth than I can imagine. Not that I need any of that. My bank account is ridiculously large. But whatever is behind the door, men and women have died fighting to protect. They have entrusted me.

I push the door open and step inside. The door automatically closes behind me, making me jump.

It's dark inside, so I flick a light on. And jump again. The room runs the entire length that Surrender once did. I can barely see to the other side. And it's filled with paintings, jewels, money and riches, none of which particularly surprises me. I see drawers of plans for future weapons. And I'm sure every technology we have ever created exists between these walls. I take my time looking at everything. I need to spend more time down here to understand it all, not because the money or riches mean anything to me, but because I need to decide what should be done with it.

Today isn't that day.

I walk back to the door and see the keypad and face scanner that will let me out. I enter the code in again and then it asks for it to be changed and my face scanned. I change the code to something ridiculous but unforgettable. This seems too important to forget. The machine scans my face, and then the door unlocks.

I'm about to leave when I see an envelope taped below it with one word on it—Black.

I grab the envelope and leave the vault, and the responsibilities of Black, behind. It's time to go to a birthday party.

———

"You invited Liesel and Langston?" Beckett asks as he carries the cake into the kitchen of our brand new Miami house. We had a new house rebuilt on the site of the final game. The site Enzo's home used to live on. It felt right. We are moving in tomorrow, but today is the twins' first birthday. So we are celebrating in our empty house first.

"Yes," I answer.

"But don't they hate each other?" he asks.

"I don't think so," I say.

"That's wishful thinking," Enzo says, scooping Finn up and tossing him over his head. Finn laughs hysterically as he flies through the air and lands in his father's arms.

"We don't know for sure. We haven't seen them in months," I say. I haven't seen Liesel since the day of the final game. And I haven't seen Langston since he walked out my door in anger.

The doorbell rings, and I scoop Ellie up. "Let's go see who's at the door."

I open it, and Langston and Liesel are both at the door holding presents with a pissed expression on their faces. *Well, I guess that answers that question.*

"Come in!" I say, cheerily. I'm so happy all the people I love are in the same room celebrating.

Ellie tugs at my black scrunchie on my wrist. My heart tugs. *Well, most of the people I love are here.*

I lead Langston and Liesel into the kitchen where they set the gifts down, and Enzo and Beckett give them both hugs and small talk.

"Cake," Finn says, motioning to his mouth. He can't say many words, but Enzo thought they should both know the word cake before their birthday.

"Ca!" Ellie says, not quite able to say the "ke" sound yet.

I smile. "I think we should do the cakes first, then open gifts."

Everyone nods. I put Ellie in her high chair while Enzo puts Finn in his. And then we carry the two small individual-sized cakes we got in front of each of them while Beckett carries the large cake and ice cream for the rest of us to the table. We all gather around and start singing happy birthday, but we didn't really think it through. Both of the kids start digging into their cakes before we are even halfway through the song. I snap a million pictures of them as they eat their cake—loving every second of this.

Beckett slices the main cake and scoops out vanilla ice cream onto each plate.

I bite my lips as Enzo takes a bite of cake with ice cream, his first time tasting the treat.

"Oh my god. This is the sweetest, most delicious thing," Enzo says.

We all laugh.

"Wait until you try other flavors. It will blow your mind," I say.

Enzo shovels more of the cake and ice cream into his mouth.

But then my phone rings. I stop to answer it. "We are under attack," Clifton says.

I sigh. "We will be right there."

I end the call. "Duty calls."

Enzo and Beckett stand up.

"Where are you going?" Liesel asks.

"One of our ships was attacked. It's thirty minutes from here. We need to make sure everyone is okay. We will be two hours tops," I say as I kiss Finn and Ellie on the head who don't care their parents have to step away from their birthday party for a couple of hours. They have cake.

"You two don't mind watching them while we are gone, do you? It will only be an hour or two. They can have all the cake they want, but don't let them open any of the gifts until we get back," I say, not really giving Liesel or Langston a choice as the three of us—Enzo, Beckett, and I, step out the door.

I shut the door, and then we climb into our Escalade. Beckett drives while Enzo rides shotgun, and I sit in the back.

"Tell me the truth, is there really an emergency or is this a setup to get Langston and Liesel to like each other again?" Enzo asks, glaring at me.

"There is a real emergency. But this could be the exact thing they need to bring them back together again," I say.

"Or drive them further apart," Enzo says.

I roll my eyes. "Always so negative."

I reach into my pocket to look at the pictures on my phone again. I'm sad we have to step away from their birthday for even a minute, but I'm happy we have finally found a good balance between keeping our family safe and running a criminal empire that does plenty of good, along with the less than legal parts of the business.

I feel the crumpled envelope in my pocket I put in my pocket after I left the vault earlier but never read.

Beckett pulls up to the docks, and we all get out.

"I'll go get a boat ready, so we can meet them," Beckett says.

Enzo and I nod.

Enzo takes my hand while I start opening the envelope. "I think we should get married. Have the fancy big wedding you've always wanted. We have our life figured out now; the kids are old enough; we have everyone we love back in our lives. We can do it at the Miami home or in Alaska if you prefer. I don't care. I just want to celebrate our love every chance we get."

He grabs my cheeks and kisses me hard and desperately, turning me on in only the way he can.

I slowly break the kiss. "We can't fuck here; we have a job to do and kids to get back to."

He shrugs. "Just getting you ready for later tonight. So what do you say? Marry me again, stingray? With our entire family and friends there?"

I pretend to think about it, but I already know I'm going to say yes. In the passionate kiss, I dropped the envelope's contents on the floor. I pick up the single sheet of paper, and the opening sentence catches my eye.

"Stingray?" Enzo asks, waiting for an answer.

I hold up a hand for him to wait a second so I can read the note.

STINGRAY,

I'M SO sorry that I'm gone. I'm sorry about the pain you are in at my loss. I'm sorry I'm not there to protect you. But I know it's for the best. If I come back, danger will follow me. And I don't want to ever put you in danger again. I will come back when it's safe. I hope you have found the love you were always meant to find. And if you are reading this, I was right, and you won the games. You are Mrs. Black. I'll send this note to Archard to give to you after you win. And if Enzo is reading this, then tell Kai I'm alive, you dipshit. If stingray is reading this, keep it to yourself. For now, I must stay dead.

LOVE,
—Z

. . .

MY EYES WATER reading the note—Zeke's alive. And just like that, my heart finishes healing. My world is whole again.

"Kai, what is it?" Enzo asks.

I consider going against Zeke and telling Enzo Zeke is alive. But I know Zeke will reappear in our lives when the time is right. Because sometimes the people we love come back from the dead. I think about my father. Sometimes they stay dead.

But I have hope Zeke will come back. We will see each other again. Our family will one day be whole again.

"Do you still have that lighter?" I ask Enzo.

He nods slowly, reaches into his pocket and hands it to me.

I light the note on fire, toss it to the sand, and I wait for it to burn to ash. I choose to let Zeke's secret stay hidden because sometimes people need to stay dead until it's safe for them to be alive again.

"What was in that note?" Enzo asks.

"Do you trust me?"

"With my life."

"Then trust you will find out when the time is right."

Enzo sighs. "I hate that I let you be the leader sometimes."

I give him side-eye. "Let me?"

"Fine, I take it back. I love that you are the queen you deserve to be. You were always meant to be Mrs. Black."

I kiss him. "That I was."

"What was in the note?" he tries again.

"It was really good," I say with a grin as we walk down the pier.

He sighs. "But you aren't going to tell me?"

"Nope. Someday, but not today."

"You are one frustrating woman."

"I know."

"So will you marry me again?"

"Someday."

He frowns. "Why not now?"

Because I want everyone I love there, including Zeke. "You'll see."

He huffs.

My phone rings, and I answer Clifton, listen to him talk for a minute, and then hang up.

"Are you going to tell me what that was about?" Enzo asks.

"That I can do. Clifton called to say they were able to handle the attack. They thought they were hauling drugs, but Clifton and the crew captured the men. We don't need to go."

"Good, because I need to punish you for not telling me why you won't marry me." He slaps me on the ass and then scoops me up in his arms. Eyeing one of our yachts docked near us, he heads in that direction.

"What about Beckett?" I ask.

"This won't take long."

"The kids?"

"They will understand." He devours my lips as he carries me onto the ship. The crew on board is used to seeing us like this and don't even bat an eye at Enzo carrying me down the stairs to use one of the bedrooms.

"Langston and Liesel?"

He shuts the door behind us as he tosses me on the bed. He shrugs. "They will probably kill each other."

I laugh as he jumps on the bed and starts removing my shirt.

"Are you ready to be punished, Mrs. Black?"

"Definitely."

He slaps my ass again before kissing me like it's the first and last time. Because with us, you never know. Danger is all around us. Every day could be our last together. So we make the most of every day.

We undress each other quickly, and Enzo is inside me thrusting in record time, slapping my ass occasionally to serve as my punishment for keeping secrets from him.

"Truth or lie, I have a cousin who wants to fight me for control of the company," I say.

I laugh as he thrusts again.

"Lie."

Another thrust.

"You have a sister who wants to fight you for custody of our kids."

"Lie."

He thrusts again, and the truth or lies game grows more serious as our orgasms grow closer together.

"Truth or lie, you love me, and our family comes before the empire."

"Always."

"Truth or lie, you trust me to keep secrets from you because I only do it to protect those we love."

"Truth, I trust you with my life, our kids, this empire. You were always the right person for the job."

"And you were always the right person for me."

Enzo thrusts again, and I come hard around his cock. But he lied earlier, when he said he was going to fuck me quick. We fuck two more times before we go find Beckett and return to the kid's birthday party. We almost always tell each other the truth. But every once in a while, we tell a lie. Because sometimes the lies protect us or those we love. Sometimes the truth does irrecoverable damage.

But whether we are telling a truth or a lie, there is one thing we both agree on—love wins.

The End

Thank you so much for reading Enzo and Kai's story! I'm currently writing more books in the Truth or Lies world! The next couple I will be writing about is Zeke & Siren! Book 1 of their series is called Sinful Truth!

Check out the blurb & preorder Zeke's story below!

PREORDER Sinful Truth HERE—Coming November 5th

She saved me.
Pulled me from the depths of the ocean.
Siren—her name fits. She is beauty; her voice is heavenly.
But unlike the myths of the sirens, Siren didn't lure me to my death.
She saved me.
And now, seeing her about to be sold to the highest bidder, I know it's my turn to save her.

PREORDER Sinful Truth HERE

P.S. I know Langston and Liesel also have a story to tell. They just like to fight their love more than most couples...

FREE BOOKS

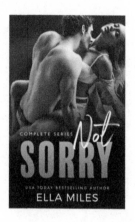

Read **Not Sorry** for **FREE**! And sign up to get my latest
releases, updates, and more goodies
here→EllaMiles.com/freebooks

Follow me on BookBub to get notified of my new releases
and recommendations here→Follow on BookBub Here

Join Ella's Bellas FB group for giveaways and FUN & a
FREE copy of **Pretend I'm Yours**→Join Ella's Bellas Here

Order Signed Paperbacks→https://ellamiles.com/signed-
paperbacks

ALSO BY ELLA MILES

TRUTH OR LIES:

DIRTY SERIES:

ALIGNED SERIES:

Aligned: The Complete Series Boxset

UNFORGIVABLE SERIES:

Heart of a Thief

Heart of a Liar

Heart of a Prick

Unforgivable: The Complete Series Boxset

MAYBE, DEFINITELY SERIES:

Maybe Yes

Maybe Never

Maybe Always

Definitely Yes

Definitely No

Definitely Forever

STANDALONES:

Pretend I'm Yours

Finding Perfect

Savage Love

Too Much

Not Sorry

ABOUT THE AUTHOR

Ella Miles writes steamy romance, including everything from dark suspense romance that will leave you on the edge of your seat to contemporary romance that will leave you laughing out loud or crying. Most importantly, she wants you to feel everything her characters feel as you read.

Ella is currently living her own happily ever after near the Rocky Mountains with her high school sweetheart husband. Her heart is also taken by her goofy five year old black lab who is scared of everything, including her own shadow.

Ella is a USA Today Bestselling Author & Top 50 Bestselling Author.

Stalk Ella at:
www.ellamiles.com
ella@ellamiles.com

Made in the USA
Coppell, TX
11 December 2022

88821312R00163